FRACTURED REUNION

A CHRISTIAN MEDICAL ROMANCE

THE MONROE FAMILY

LAURA SCOTT

CHAPTER ONE

Dr. Aaron Monroe froze when he recognized his ex-wife, Maggie Dall, off to one side of the large conference room of the very fancy Pfister Hotel in Milwaukee, Wisconsin. What in the world was she doing there?

Silly question. Obviously, they were both attending the same medical conference. But he hadn't seen Maggie in two years.

Two years, one week, and five days, if he were being honest. The worst day of his life, the finalization of their divorce, was etched in his memory forever.

Maggie laughed at something, tucking a strand of her long, dark curly hair behind her ear. His heart clenched, making him wonder for the millionth time if Maggie had found someone else.

Maybe even remarried.

Started a family.

The sting of regret was sharp. Their marriage had ended over their inability to have children. Maggie had walked away, and Aaron had let her go.

But he hadn't recovered from their split. And doubted he ever would.

Oh, he'd told himself to get over her. She was the one who'd left him. He'd tried to move on, had even left his position as a pediatric cardiac surgeon at Johns Hopkins to return to Milwaukee to be closer to his family. His dad's heart attack had been the primary motivation for the move.

But he'd also thought it would be the best way to avoid running into Maggie as she worked for Johns Hopkins too.

Ironic to run into her here in their hometown.

She moved toward the doors leading outside. For reasons he couldn't name, he quickly crossed the room to follow. Even though there were plenty of conference attendees that he could use as a buffer, he wanted to talk to her.

To see if she was remarried.

He hadn't noticed her name of Maggie Dall on the list of attendees. Maybe once he knew for sure she had remarried, he would also be able to move on with his life.

"Maggie?" He pushed through the door. The bright autumn sun flickered off the yellow and gold leaves on the trees.

Maggie turned to face him. Her brown eyes held his gaze, but she didn't look surprised to see him. He was one of the conference presenters after all. She couldn't really pretend to not have noticed his name and professional photo on the website.

Was that why she'd come? To see him?

Don't go there, he silently warned. Yet he couldn't quite squash the surge of hope when he saw her name tag read Maggie Dall.

"Hi, Aaron. How have you been?" Her polite tone put his teeth on edge. A quick glance at her left hand revealed she was not wearing a ring.

Which didn't mean much these days.

"I'm doing well, thanks." That was a big fat lie, but there was no sense dredging up the past. "How about you?"

"I'm good." The stilted conversation could not have been more awkward. "I heard you relocated to Milwaukee. How do you like working at Children's Memorial?"

"It's great." Why on earth had he followed her outside? This chitchat was pure torture. "My dad had a heart attack in the spring, and while he's doing fine now, I decided it was time to be closer to the family."

"Of course, you'd want to be near them. I'm glad your dad is doing okay."

Maggie had always liked his family, which made it that much worse when she'd walked away from their marriage. Aaron was the oldest of six, and they all worked in the medical field in some way. Except for his brother Alec who was a police detective. They often teased Alec that his lack of being a doctor was why he'd married a physician named Jillian.

"Well, I just wanted to say hi." He forced a smile as if seeing her wasn't ripping his heart from his chest.

"Aaron—" She was interrupted by a loud crash. He looked to the right, horrified to see that a large truck had T-boned a city bus.

Without hesitation, he ran toward the scene of the crash. Maggie quickly joined him.

"Get back! We're doctors! Call 911 and get back!" He shoved gawkers out of the way to reach the bus. Peering through the door, he could see the driver was bleeding from a cut on his head, but otherwise, he was conscious. When Aaron pounded on the door, he opened it.

"I—don't know what happened," the driver stuttered.

"I know. We're doctors and are here to help," Maggie said from behind him.

Ignoring the screams and crying from the passengers wasn't easy. He immediately focused on the right side of the bus where the truck had slammed into it. That side had sustained the most damage.

"If you're not hurt, get off the bus," he said in a stern tone. "We're doctors here to help those who are injured." He didn't want to be sidetracked by people who were panicked but otherwise physically okay.

He stopped at the seat two rows behind the driver where a man was cradling his bloody arm. The extremity was clearly fractured, and the patient seemed to be fading in and out of consciousness.

Bending over the injured man, he checked for a pulse. Present but erratic enough to indicate he may have suffered heart damage too. He glanced over to where Maggie had stopped at the next set of passengers, a woman holding her young son.

"She's not breathing and doesn't have a pulse," Maggie said, her gaze stricken.

The little boy clung to his mother, sobbing. Maggie gently pulled him away from the injured woman, and instantly the child wrapped his arms tightly around her neck.

"Let me get her on the floor so I can start CPR." He moved on from the gentleman with the broken arm to provide life-saving treatment to the woman without a pulse.

Maggie and the little boy scooted back so he could place the woman on the floor of the narrow aisle between the seats. He double-checked to make sure she didn't have a pulse before starting CPR.

To his surprise, Maggie shifted the little boy in her arms to kneel at the woman's head. "I'll hold her airway."

"Check the others first," he said between compressions. "I've got this."

"Okay." Maggie turned to begin examining the other crash victims even while the little boy clung to her like a monkey. The child had stopped crying but seemed as if he was determined not to let Maggie go.

Seeing them together only reinforced the reason their marriage had failed. Maggie was a natural with kids and deserved to be a mother.

His thoughts were interrupted by the arrival of the first responders. He waited as the first crew of EMTs took the man with the shattered arm out first, leaving the second pair of EMTs to assist with his injured woman.

"Keep doing CPR while we get her connected to the AED," the one paramedic said.

He didn't announce his profession as a cardiac surgeon. Right now, they were all doing their best to save the lives of these patients.

Glancing toward the rear of the bus, he noticed another pair of EMTs had come in through the rear door. They were assisting another patient that Maggie had been caring for. When they had the situation under control, Maggie moved back, cradling the little boy.

She looked at him expectantly, clearly hoping that the child's mother would survive.

"Okay, stop CPR so we can do a rhythm check," the paramedic said.

Aaron sat back on his heels, eyeing the monitor. The straight line across the screen was not good.

Asystole.

He had a bad feeling this woman had died on impact.

"Stay back," the paramedic said. "I'll deliver a shock in case this is fine V-fib."

It wasn't, but Aaron didn't argue. Delivering a series of shocks might help. And if not, she would be just as dead.

Three shocks later, the straight line across the monitor was unchanged.

"Continue CPR," the paramedic said.

"There's no need. I'm Dr. Aaron Monroe, a cardiac surgeon with Children's Memorial. I'm calling this code. We can document the time of death as ten forty-five a.m."

The two paramedics looked at each other, then shrugged. "We'll need you to sign the paperwork, Dr. Monroe," the red-haired paramedic said. His name tag read Finnegan, and Aaron vaguely remembered meeting a Dr. Faye Finnegan. Possibly related, but no way to know for sure.

"No problem," he assured him. He glanced over to where Maggie sat with the little boy on her lap. Her stricken expression stabbed deep.

Aaron sighed and dropped his chin to his chest, knowing he'd failed her.

Again.

MAGGIE DALL CUDDLED the frightened boy close, wishing she could assure the child he would be fine. But his mother had just died, and from this moment on, this little boy's life would be changed forever.

Dear Lord, please have mercy on this child!

"What's your name?" she asked, smoothing a reassuring hand down the child's back. She estimated he was between three and four years old, and a little too scrawny for her piece of mind. "Can you tell me your name?"

He shook his head, burying closer to her. His arms were wrapped tightly around her neck as if he'd never let her go.

Did he somehow sense his mother was gone? That his world had been turned upside down?

"We'll have to get Child Protective Services involved," Aaron said. "He may have a father or other family."

"I know." She squelched a flash of anger. It wasn't Aaron's fault that this had happened. He'd done everything he could, performing CPR and delivering shocks to save the little boy's mother's life.

"My name is Maggie," she said to the little boy. "Can you say Maggie?"

The child shook his head again, gripping her tighter. So much so that she had to shift his hold so he wouldn't cut off her airway.

"His mother's name is Pamela Johnson," Aaron said. "Her address is an apartment in Milwaukee. I'm sure the police will head over to see if there are other family members there."

"Okay, but I'm going to ride along to the hospital with him." She couldn't have pried the little boy's arms from around her neck if she'd wanted to. "He needs a full assessment to evaluate for internal injuries." The fact that his mother had died as a result of the crash concerned her that the child was hurt too.

"I'll go with you," Aaron offered.

She frowned. "That's not necessary. Don't you have a presentation to give?"

He glanced at his watch. "Yes, but after lunch, so I have a few hours."

When Maggie had signed up for the Midwest Cardiac

Surgery Medical Symposium, she'd known her ex-husband was one of the esteemed presenters. But she honestly had not expected him to seek her out.

The two years since their divorce had been difficult. She had been the one to initiate the filing, but she'd done that for him, not for her.

She was the one who couldn't have children. Aaron came from a large family, and she knew how much he'd wanted to carry on the Monroe name. She'd told herself she was doing the right thing by letting Aaron find someone else to share his life with.

Yet to her knowledge, he hadn't.

And now that she was face-to-face with him again, she realized her heart still ached for what she'd given up.

"Ma'am?" An EMT touched her arm. "We can take the boy now."

"I'm Dr. Maggie Dall, a pediatric anesthesiologist," she said. "I'm going to the hospital with him."

"Oh, uh, sure." The EMT wasn't about to override a physician's decision. "Please come with me."

She nodded and stood. Suddenly Aaron was there with his hand beneath her elbow to help steady her. She hoped he didn't notice the tremor that rippled through her body at his touch.

"I'll meet you at Children's Memorial," Aaron said, after helping her into the ambulance.

"Only if you have time." She forced herself to give him an out. "You have a presentation to prepare for, so I'll understand if you can't make it."

"I'll meet you there," Aaron repeated, a stubborn glint in his green eyes. Then he stepped back so the EMT could shut the ambulance doors.

The little boy relaxed his tight grip as if sensing he was

safe. She continued stroking a hand down his back, whispering reassurances. Then she gently palpated his limbs.

He didn't appear to be in pain. But he also wasn't talking, so she wasn't even sure he could understand her. The child didn't look Hispanic, but that didn't mean he'd been exposed to the English language.

The little boy cried out in pain as her hand passed over his side toward his abdomen.

"Does that hurt?" she asked.

He nodded and pressed closer to her.

At least he understood that much. "I'm Doctor Maggie. What's your name?"

He didn't respond.

The ambulance ride to Children's Memorial Hospital located right next to Trinity Medical Center didn't take long. When the EMT opened the back, she carried the little boy down and into the emergency department.

"Who do we have here?" the friendly woman at the front desk asked.

"I'm Dr. Maggie Dall, pediatric anesthesiologist, and this is a young victim of the bus crash outside the Pfister Hotel. Unfortunately, I don't know his name."

The woman frowned. "Where is his parent or guardian?"

"Not here." Maggie didn't want to say the word *dead* in front of the boy. "I know his last name is Johnson, and he needs to be scanned for internal bleeding. He has tenderness on the right side of his abdomen, could be a lacerated liver."

It looked as if the woman might argue, but just then she felt someone come up to stand beside her.

"Dr. Aaron Monroe," he said, introducing himself. "We need a room for this child ASAP."

"Of course, Dr. Monroe. This way." The woman stood and led them through a doorway into the emergency department.

The fact that her title hadn't garnered the same respect made Maggie cranky, but she held her tongue. How they'd gotten through to the back didn't matter; providing this little boy the medical care he needed did.

"I need you to lie down on the cot," she told the child.

He shook his head, gripping her tighter. Her heart ached for him, but she had to be able to examine him.

"Please, for me," she cajoled, trying to gently pry his arms from the locked hold he had on her neck. "I won't leave you. I'll stay right here with you, okay?"

He shook his head again but then relaxed his grip. "You'll stay?"

They were the first words he'd uttered since she'd found him, and she bent her head to meet his gaze. "Yes. I'll stay. I promise. I won't leave you."

He nodded, then put his hand on his abdomen. "Hurts."

"I understand, we're going to find out why your tummy hurts and make it all better, okay?" She smiled reassuringly, thrilled the boy was finally talking. "I'm Dr. Maggie, and I'm going to help take care of you. What's your name?"

There was a long pause as he gazed up at her. "Joey."

"I love the name Joey. Can you tell me if you hurt anywhere else?" She didn't see any other obvious signs of an injury. "Your head? Your arms or legs?"

"My tummy," he said. "Hurts."

"Okay." She glanced at Aaron who stood near the door, watching her interact with their young patient. When the nurse came over with a hospital gown, she took the garment from her. "Joey, can we take your shirt and pants off to put this gown on?"

"No. Don't wanna." His lower lip trembled. "I want my mommy."

"Oh, sweetheart, I know you do." She gathered him close, wishing more than anything she could present his mother.

But his mother was gone and never coming back. Something she'd have to explain to the boy sooner or later. Maybe after he'd gotten his scans to make sure he wasn't bleeding internally. "He can stay in his clothes for a CT scan, right?" she said to the nurse.

The nurse glanced from Maggie to Aaron, then nodded. "Sure. If that's what you want."

"Let's get the CT scan ordered so we know what we're dealing with," Aaron said. Again, the nurses acted as if he were the doctor in charge rather than the pediatric emergency medicine physician hovering nearby, who appeared to be deferring all decisions to Aaron.

Apparently, Aaron Monroe was the big cheese around here. Good for him.

They were able to create a new medical record for the boy under the name of Joseph Johnson. She sank into the closest chair, holding Joey on her lap as the emergency department doc spoke with Aaron and entered orders using the computer mounted on a rolling stand in the opposite corner of the room. While waiting, she was far too conscious of Aaron's penetrating gaze.

There was so much emotional baggage between them she was surprised he was here. Especially when he had the excuse of being a presenter at the medical conference. The way he'd jumped in to help those injured in the crash reminded her of the man she used to know.

The man she'd fallen in love with.

Doing her best to ignore Aaron and their fractured past,

she focused her attention on the little boy in her arms. She was content to hold him, to stay with him.

To get him through this.

She hated the idea of Joey ending up in the foster system. As she soothed the child, she silently hoped and prayed Joey didn't have anything seriously wrong with him.

And that he had other family members who would soon arrive at the hospital to help take care of him.

CHAPTER TWO

Watching Maggie hold Joey was heartbreaking. She so deserved to be a mother, and Aaron resented God for not allowing Maggie to live her dream. Yet when he had suggested adopting, Maggie had refused.

Looking at her cradling the little boy now made him wonder if she might change her mind.

Not that it mattered. She'd walked away from their vows, their marriage, and their love.

Enough. He had to stop torturing himself over the demise of his marriage. His parents had been together for over forty years, and it was difficult for him to accept that he'd failed when it came to having the same type of relationship they had.

A wonderful, supportive, and enduring one.

Apparently, that was not meant to be for him. Aaron straightened when a tech entered the room. "I'm here to take a patient named Joseph Johnson to the CT scanner?"

"Right here." Maggie pushed herself up off the chair while still holding on to Joey. "Lead the way."

The tech appeared disconcerted but then turned to

leave. Maggie gave him a quick nod as she passed. Maybe a thank you for getting Joey the care he needed.

As if he'd stand by and do nothing for the little boy who'd lost his mother.

He glanced at his watch, wincing at the time. Even though he'd asked for the radiology scan to be expedited, he would have to leave soon if he was going to make his presentation.

As the Chairman of Pediatric Cardiac Surgery, he didn't think skipping the program was wise. He was relatively new in his role, and his being promoted above other cardiac surgeons with more experience had not necessarily gone over well. Yet he didn't want to leave until he knew Joey wasn't badly injured. If the boy was bleeding into his abdomen, he might need surgery depending on the size of the hematoma.

Aaron reached for his phone, scrolling through his list of contacts until he found the one he wanted. Dr. Kyle Flores was the best pediatric trauma surgeon on staff. He called his colleague, hoping the guy wasn't in the OR.

To his surprise, Kyle answered. "What's up? I thought you were doing a presentation at the Pfister?"

"Yeah, soon. I responded to a bus crash outside the hotel. We have a four-year-old by the name of Joseph Johnson with abdominal pain getting a CT scan right now. I'd like you to take a look at the results, see what you think."

"I heard something about that," Kyle said. "I'm between cases, so I can head down now."

"Thanks." He pocketed his phone and walked out into the hustle and bustle of the emergency department. When he saw Kyle Flores stroll in, Aaron hurried over to meet him.

"They're down the hall in radiology."

Kyle nodded, and by mutual agreement, they headed in that direction. Aaron could hear Maggie speaking with Joey from the hallway as they approached.

"You're very brave, Joey. I'm so proud of you. Just continue to lie still, okay? That way we can get pictures of your tummy."

"Can I see the pictures?" Joey asked.

"I don't think so because they won't look like pictures in a book," Maggie said. "They're pictures only the doctors can understand."

"Hurts," Joey whimpered.

"Please hold still," the tech said from his position behind the console. There was a lead-glass partition separating the CT scanner itself from the area where the tech reviews the images on screen. As he and Kyle entered the image room, he wasn't surprised to see Maggie was sitting in a chair beside Joey who was lying on the CT table.

"Just a little while longer," Maggie said encouragingly. "Maybe I can read you a story when you're finished. Would you like that?"

Aaron stood off to the side giving Kyle room to see the images displayed on the screen. There were dual monitors, so while the tech continued his job of obtaining the next set of pictures, Kyle pulled up the images that had already been completed.

"I see the hematoma," Kyle said. "Looks to be three centimeters in diameter in this image, but I'll need the rest to make a final determination."

"Would you recommend taking it out?" Aaron asked.

"If it's as big as I think it is, based on these initial images, yes. I'll want the radiology report finalized, though, before I go in."

"Are you sure you'll have time today?" Aaron trusted

Kyle, but if time was of the essence, he couldn't very well expect the trauma surgeon to push off a procedure he'd already scheduled.

"Yes, I can take Joey after my next procedure." Kyle eyed the little boy through the lead glass. "Is that his mother?"

"No, that's Dr. Maggie Dall. She's a pediatric anesthesiologist from Johns Hopkins," Aaron explained. "She responded to the crash site with me. Unfortunately, Joey's mother died in the crash."

Kyle frowned. "I'll need to get consent from a family member," he said. "From these initial images, I can't say that taking him to the OR is a matter of life and death to bypass the need for a surgical consent."

Aaron grimaced and nodded. "The police were going to see if they could find any family at the address listed on his mother's ID. But what if they can't? I don't want to delay his care."

Kyle sighed. "I'm not sure. I might have to run this up the administrative flagpole."

Eyeing Maggie speaking softly to Joey, Aaron knew that response would not go over well. Hospital administrators were not known for making quick decisions. Especially if they had to get their hospital attorneys involved.

"I guess that's up to you," he finally said. "I just hope that the administrative delay doesn't hurt the little boy."

"Look, I need to get back to the OR," Kyle said with a sigh. "I'll put Joey here tentatively on my schedule to follow the next case, but I'll have to see the final results before I can move forward. I might be able to make an argument for considering this procedure emergent, but it would be easier all around if the police can find a parent or close relative to act as a legal guardian for this kid."

"I will see what I can do." He tore his gaze from Maggie and Joey. "I appreciate you coming down so quickly."

"Anytime. Keep in touch." Kyle nodded and left.

If Aaron was going to make his presentation, he'd need to hit the road soon. He could follow up with the police on his way back to the hotel. Maybe knowing the little boy needed surgery would help spur things along.

He considered calling Alec, his brother the detective, but decided to hold off. He could always use his brother as leverage later if his attempt to go through official channels didn't work.

He stepped into the CT scanner. "Maggie?"

She turned to face him, her brown eyes reflecting surprise. "You're still here? I thought you'd left."

"I'm heading out now. Just wanted to let you know that a trauma surgeon colleague of mine, Kyle Flores, will be reviewing Joey's CT scan results when they're available. He has him tentatively placed on the OR schedule for later this afternoon, depending on what the final results show."

"Kyle Flores, got it," Maggie said. "Thanks for doing that."

"Of course. I have to head back to the hotel, but I'll check back with you and Joey later." He hesitated, then decided not to get into the issue of Joey's guardianship. There would be time to tackle that issue if the police hadn't found anyone at Pamela Johnson's address.

"Good luck with your presentation, but don't worry about us. We're fine," Maggie said, before turning back to Joey.

He knew that was her way of saying she didn't need his ongoing support. It was a bit like a slap in the face, especially since she was wrong about that. For once, having the title of Chairman of Pediatric Cardiac Surgery might be useful, rather than just a whole lot of additional paperwork and meetings.

If there was a way to get Joey the surgery he needed, Aaron fully intended to make that happen. No matter whose feathers he had to ruffle in the process.

MAGGIE WAS TOUCHED by how Aaron had gone the extra mile in finding a pediatric trauma surgeon to follow up with Joey's injury. Obviously, she wouldn't have married him in the first place if he'd been an arrogant jerk. Even as he'd earned a reputation for being a highly sought-after pediatric cardiac surgeon, he hadn't let his success go to his head.

Most of the time. On occasion, she'd had to reel him back in.

Yet their relationship had grown strained as they'd undergone one set of infertility testing after another. A tension that had finally reached its breaking point when she'd been forced to accept that she would never be able to give birth to Aaron's child.

That she would not be able to contribute to the next generation in the Monroe family.

"Hold still," the tech said again.

She shook off the useless thoughts of the past. She and Aaron weren't together anymore. She had no doubt that he'd moved on, especially after he'd relocated back to his hometown. Besides, there were more important things to focus on. Like this poor child who likely had suffered internal bleeding after being in the bus crash. She leaned forward, resting her hand on the little boy's head. "Lie still,

Joey, okay? Just for a few more minutes. We're almost finished taking pictures of your tummy."

The little boy squirmed but then nodded. He was trying so hard to please her. She couldn't imagine how she'd find the words to tell him his mother was never coming back.

Tears stung her eyes just thinking about it.

"Okay, three more pictures to go," the tech said.

"You're being such a good boy," she whispered to Joey.

"Where's my mommy?" Joey had asked this question three times now, and she still had no idea how to answer him.

"I know your mommy was on the bus with you, but where was your daddy?" she asked. "Was he at work?"

"No, I don't have a daddy. Just Mommy." His lower lip quivered again. "I want my mommy."

"Shh, it's okay. I'm here." She hoped the tech would hurry up with the last three pictures. "I won't leave you, Joey. I promise."

It seemed like an eternity before the tech finally said, "We're all set. You can get up off the table now, Joey."

"Easy, though," she cautioned, unsure of the CT scan results. She assumed Joey had a hematoma, but it could be small, large, or somewhere in between. She eased the boy into her arms and stood. "I'll carry him back to his room."

"Sure thing. I'll show you the way." The radiology tech took a long hallway back to the busy emergency department. He led the way to their previous room. "I've sent the scan images to the radiologist. I'm sure the physicians here will be able to see the results soon."

"Great, thank you." She lowered herself into the chair, keeping Joey on her lap. The hour was close to lunchtime, but Joey couldn't have anything to eat or drink if he was scheduled for surgery.

For long minutes, no one entered the room. It made Maggie wonder if the staff didn't care anymore about Joey now that Aaron wasn't there. She was about to stand and reach for the nursing call light when the previous nurse breezed into the room.

"I'm sorry, I didn't catch your name," Maggie said. The nurse's name tag was turned backward so she couldn't read it.

"I'm Rachel. I'll be here until seven o'clock this evening," Rachel said.

Maggie knew twelve-hour shifts were rapidly becoming the norm, albeit with mixed feedback. Twelve hours was a long time for a nurse to be on his or her feet caring for patients. Yet longer shifts also meant an extra day or two off each week or pay period.

"Hi, Rachel. Would you be able to let me know when the radiology report on Joey's CT scan is ready? I'd like to read the results for myself."

"Oh, uh, sure." Rachel looked confused for a moment. "Are you on staff here too? Like Dr. Monroe?"

"I'm a pediatric anesthesiologist from Johns Hopkins," she said. "Aaron is—an old friend of mine. We both responded to the bus crash."

"Got it," Rachel said with a smile. "Okay, I'll let you know. In the meantime, we have Joey listed as NPO." Maggie knew that meant nothing by mouth. "Dr. Flores has him tentatively on the OR schedule for three p.m. this afternoon."

"I understand." Telling Joey that he couldn't have food and water would not be easy. "Thanks for the update."

"Yeah, sure." Rachel nodded at Joey. "I'll need to get a set of vitals on him."

"Of course." She shifted the little boy in her lap. "Joey,

Nurse Rachel is going to listen to your heart and your breathing, okay?"

He shrugged but didn't protest when Rachel wrapped a pediatric-sized blood pressure cuff around his arm. He handled the procedure like a trouper. A few minutes later, Rachel stepped back.

"His blood pressure and pulse are a bit high, likely because of his belly pain," Rachel said. She turned to log into the computer in the corner of the room to document her findings. "But he's otherwise stable."

"Thank you." Maggie settled back in her seat, wondering what would happen next. She didn't care about missing the rest of the conference, that was the least of her worries. She'd only signed up in the first place because all physicians needed continuing educational credits and she'd been behind in getting her educational sessions in.

But it felt strange to sit here with Joey without knowing what was going on with the rest of the bus crash victims.

Most of them had been relatively unharmed. As Aaron had performed CPR on Pamela Johnson, she'd gone through the rest of the bus to check on the other passengers. Two had sustained broken arms, including the man who'd been sitting relatively close to the bus driver. That man had sustained a concussion, too, as had another victim behind the seat where she'd found Pamela and Joey. Thankfully, none of the other passengers had sustained a life-threatening injury.

Unlike Joey's mother. It was difficult not to question God's plan. She didn't want to give the child the horrible news about his mother's passing without having something more to offer. Like his aunt, uncle, or someone who would be stepping in to take care of him.

Surely this little boy wasn't completely alone in this world.

Was he?

The minutes ticked by slowly as she thought about Aaron giving his presentation. She already knew he was a dynamic speaker, having heard him give presentations while they were married.

She still wasn't sure what had possessed her to attend this particular conference. At some level, she must have thought it would be a good idea to get Aaron out of her head and her heart once and for all.

Yeah, that wasn't exactly how things had worked out.

Her stomach rumbled with hunger, but she ignored the sensation. Joey hadn't asked for anything to eat, and she wasn't sure if that was good or bad.

Rachel popped her head in a few minutes later. "Everything okay?" she asked.

Not really, but Maggie didn't say that. "I may need to borrow a phone to make a few calls." She didn't have her purse or her phone with her; they were back at the hotel. "I need to contact the police to see where things are at with the bus crash victims."

It took Rachel a second to understand. Then the nurse nodded. "Of course, I understand. I think we have a few landline phones left. I'll see if I can find one for you."

"Thanks." It was difficult not to feel naked without a phone, a wallet, even a credit card.

She didn't have long to wait, as Rachel returned fifteen minutes later, but instead of a phone, she escorted a heavyset police officer. "Dr. Dall, this is Officer Thomas. He has a few questions to ask."

"Nice to meet you, Officer Thomas." Maggie tried to get a hint as to the news he had to share. "This is Joey Johnson."

"Yes, I heard." The officer's eyes were kind. He came farther into the room, then hunkered down beside them. "I'd like to ask Joey a few questions if that's okay."

"Of course." She couldn't help pressing a kiss to the top of Joey's head. "Joey, can you answer some questions for the policeman?"

Joey nodded without saying anything. He still rested against her, but some of the little boy's earlier spunk was gone. She hoped it was more that he was worn out from all the activity rather than the hematoma getting worse.

"Joey, I went to the apartment where you and your mommy live, but no one was home. Do you know where your daddy is?" Officer Thomas asked.

Maggie bit her lip to prevent herself from answering for the boy.

"Don't have a daddy," Joey said. "Just my mommy."

"I see. Do you have an auntie? Or an uncle?" Officer Thomas persisted. "Brothers or sisters? Maybe in school?"

Joey shook his head. "No, just my mommy. Where is she? Can you bring my mommy here?"

The officer's compassionate gaze met hers. She shook her head, indicating she hadn't told Joey about his mother.

Officer Thomas gave a subtle nod in return. For a moment, she hoped he'd have good news to share. Then his expression turned grave as he addressed the little boy. "Joey, I'm afraid your mommy can't come here to see you." The officer's words were gentle, but they stabbed Maggie like a knife.

Tears blurred her vision, and she held the boy closer.

"Does her tummy hurt too?" Joey asked.

"No, sweetie," Maggie said, brushing her lips against his forehead. "Your mommy went to heaven to be with Jesus."

Joey frowned. "Without me?"

Dear Lord, why was this so hard? She hated every minute of giving this innocent little boy bad news but forced herself to continue. Officer Thomas had started this; it was up to her to help. "Your mommy didn't have a choice, sweetie. She died and went to heaven. I know she didn't want to leave you—" Her voice broke, and she couldn't finish.

"Yes, we know your mommy loved you very much," Officer Thomas said, picking up the discussion. "But as, er, Maggie said, she died and went to heaven. So now we're trying to find your daddy. I need your help with that, Joey. Do you know your daddy's name? Anything about him? Does he have a job? Does he live here or somewhere else?"

From Officer Thomas's questions, it was clear he had not found any close family members to step up and take care of the little boy. The knot in her stomach tightened, knowing this child might very well be all alone in the world.

Joey shook his head and then began to sob. "I want my mommy! I want my mommy!"

He repeated the phrase between jagged sobs as Maggie cried right along with him.

CHAPTER THREE

Aaron was so preoccupied by the situation with Maggie and Joey that he was certain he'd given the worst presentation of his career. At least he hadn't been booed off the stage or gotten bizarre looks from the crowd.

Then again, maybe he had gotten odd looks but hadn't noticed. Whatever. He wasn't concerned about that now. The moment he was finished, he bolted out of the hotel conference room and quickly took the grand staircase down to the main lobby level. He didn't have a room since he lived locally, but as he passed the front desk, it occurred to him that Maggie probably had a room and luggage.

What about a handbag? Or other personal items?

Thinking back, he realized she hadn't had any of her personal items with her when they'd attended to the bus crash victims.

He turned and headed back upstairs to the grand ball-room. Sweeping his gaze over the area, he spied an empty seat with a large black computer bag sitting on the floor beneath the table. He strode over to remove the bag, taking a moment to look inside.

Seeing Maggie's familiar handwriting on a notepad was a jolt.

After double-checking to make sure her phone was inside as well, he carried the bag out of the room and to his car. He was glad to be able to do this much for her and was anxious to know what was happening with Joey.

Kyle hadn't called him about taking the boy to surgery, but it was only two o'clock in the afternoon. The boy wasn't tentatively on the schedule until three. And Aaron knew how easily a routine procedure could end up being anything but uncomplicated.

He'd called the local police after leaving Maggie and Joey at the hospital. The officer he'd spoken with had assured him that they'd follow up with Joey Johnson's family. He hadn't contacted his brother Alec yet, but he was next on the list if the local police weren't any further along in finding the boy a parent or guardian.

He used the physician's parking lot at Children's Memorial even though he was not technically on duty today. His next cardiac surgical procedure was scheduled for the following week, and as today was Friday, he had hoped to have the weekend off.

But if something urgent came up, his colleagues knew to call him. Days off were somewhat of a misnomer in the world of medicine. Especially for those in leadership roles.

He'd thought his attempt to bury himself in his career would distract him from his failed marriage. One chance meeting with his ex-wife had proven him wrong. Shaking his head at his own foolishness, he grabbed her oversized handbag and headed inside.

Finding Maggie and Joey was easy enough as they were still sitting in the emergency department room they'd been in before he'd left. He frowned when he found Joey asleep on the cot and Maggie sitting with her face in her hands. When she lifted her head to look at him, it was clear she'd been crying.

Her brown eyes widened when she saw her bag. She reached for it, then stood to draw him from the room.

"What happened?" He searched her gaze. "Is Joey still having surgery?"

"I don't know about that, but the police were here. An Officer Thomas told me that he has not found anyone related to Joey. At least not yet. We tried to question the boy, but he claims he doesn't have a father, aunts, or uncles." Her gaze was stricken. "Then we had to tell him his mother was dead and never coming back. I've had to give bad news to parents before but telling that sweet boy his mother had died and went to heaven was the hardest thing I've ever done. I'm heartbroken for him."

"Ah, Maggie. I'm so sorry." Her damp puffy eyes were evidence of how badly that conversation had gone. His arms itched to draw her close the way he used to.

Before their divorce.

He made a move toward her but stopped when she reached up to rub her temple. "I'm not sure what will happen with the surgery now that he doesn't have a parent or guardian to give consent."

"Kyle was concerned about that," he admitted. "Unless he can say the procedure is emergent, meaning loss of life or limb within twenty-four hours, he'll have to wait until the court provides a temporary guardian."

"And how long does that usually take?"

He grimaced. "Not sure. Being a Friday doesn't work in our favor. I doubt the courts are in session over the weekend."

"Then let's get the wheels in motion now." Maggie's

eyes flashed with urgency. "We can't afford to wait. What if his condition deteriorates?"

He understood her concern. "I'll go to the hospital leadership with this, but what exactly did the police say? Are they still looking for his family?"

"Yes, and the social worker has also contacted Child Protective Services." She frowned. "I know they'll want to put him into emergency foster placement, but I'm not sure how that works if he needs surgery."

He wasn't an expert on this sort of thing either but remembered his brother Adam's wife Krista had gone through the process of becoming a foster parent prior to their engagement. "I'll make a few calls. Give me some time to work through my connections."

"Of course. I—uh, you have my number, right?" She flushed, then said, "I hope my phone is still in my bag."

"It is; I checked." He rested his hand on her arm. "We'll get through this, Maggie. There's always a way."

"Thanks for your help." She tucked her hair behind her ear. "I forgot to ask, how did your presentation go?"

"Fine." He waved a hand. "Not important now. Stay here with Joey, I'll let you know what I find out."

"Okay." She managed a wan smile. "I had planned on staying with Joey no matter what Child Protective Services says."

He wasn't surprised. Maggie could be doggedly stubborn when she believed she was in the right.

As evidenced by their divorce.

Aaron turned away and reached for his phone. He decided it would be easiest to head for his office to make the calls. For one thing, it was quieter than standing in the middle of the emergency department.

And for another, he felt certain he'd have to use everything he had to his advantage. Including his role as Chairman of Pediatric Cardiac Surgery.

MAGGIE WAS surprised Aaron had returned right after his presentation. Not only that, but he'd found her bag and brought that along too. He was being so sweet and considerate she was having trouble remembering their arguments.

Maybe because for the first time in years, they were on the same side of an issue. One little boy had pulled them together in a joint effort to get him the care he needed.

Ironic that an orphaned boy had brought them together when her inability to conceive had torn them apart. God worked in mysterious ways, but in this case, she would rather have had Joey's mother sitting there, alive and well.

Joey stirred on the cot, so she quickly went over to place a hand on his arm. "Shh, it's okay. You're fine."

Thankfully, the child settled back down. After crying himself to sleep, the little boy had woken several times complaining of pain in his belly. The nurse had finally obtained an order for pain medicine, and that had helped.

Maggie had asked for a copy of the CT scan report, and the images confirmed a three-by-four-centimeter hematoma. She wasn't an expert in pediatric trauma surgery but suspected that if Joey's mother was there and able to give consent, the child would already be in the OR to have it removed.

But she wasn't. And Maggie couldn't give consent in the absence of a parent. So here they sat, waiting for—what? The court to decide who could make decisions for the child?

As an anesthesiologist, she wasn't usually involved in this sort of thing. Surgeons must face this dilemma on a regular basis, but she only became involved once they had someone to give consent.

She didn't much like being on this end of the bedside.

A coughing child from two rooms over caught her attention. She left Joey's room to look inside, expecting to see someone with the child, but there was no one sitting at the little girl's bedside.

The little girl coughed again with a suspiciously croupy sound. Frowning, Maggie went into the room and pushed the call button.

Less than thirty seconds later, a nurse rushed into the room. Not Rachel, Joey's nurse, but a male nurse. "Sorry about that. I was tied up in another emergency."

"I'm not the child's guardian, but she sounds like she has croup. You may want to get her in a croup tent."

"Are you a doctor on staff?" the male nurse asked. His name was Greg, and he seemed nice enough.

"No, but I am a physician." She shot one more glance at the coughing girl as she edged toward the door.

"I'll call the resident about that croup tent," Greg promised.

She nodded and hurried back to Joey's room. She knew better than most that healthcare facilities were short-staffed these days, more so since the pandemic. Yet that didn't make her feel any better when it came to Joey getting the care he needed.

Would a court-appointed guardian sit at the little boy's bedside? Make sure he was comfortable and call the nurse if his condition changed?

Probably not.

"Mommy," Joey whined, still half asleep.

She pulled the chair closer to his cot and leaned over to

stroke his back. "It's okay. You're fine. I'm here," she whispered.

The little boy moved restlessly but then quieted under her soothing touch.

She wondered if Aaron was getting anywhere with the hospital administrators. He hadn't called her, but she belatedly realized she'd put her phone on silent during the conference. Reaching into her bag, she pulled out her phone and turned the ringer back on but then made sure to lower the volume so as not to disturb Joey.

No missed calls from Aaron, she thought with a sigh. Although to be fair, he hadn't been gone for long. She tucked the phone beneath her thigh so it was well within reach before resting her hand on Joey's back.

Then she frowned. Was it her imagination, or did the little boy feel warmer than before?

Concerned, she reached for the wall thermometer. Hoping he wouldn't wake up, she gently placed the tip of the ear probe into his ear. A moment later, a reading popped up on the screen.

His temperature was 100.8 Fahrenheit.

When Rachel had first taken Joey's vital signs, his temperature had been normal. While this temperature reading wasn't scary high, it could mean the child's body wasn't responding well to the hematoma.

If the pocket of blood became infected, the issue of parental consent would be moot. The surgery to remove it would be considered an emergency.

She would rather they didn't wait for that to happen. She grabbed her phone just as it rang. Seeing Aaron's name on the screen, she didn't hesitate to answer. "This is Maggie."

"I've asked the hospital administrator to get the lawyers

on the phone with the judge about an emergency guardian hearing," he said. "I'll be honest, Maggie, it doesn't look good that this will happen today. They're talking about having the hearing on Monday morning."

"Joey's running a fever of 100.8," she said, keeping her tone low so as not to wake the child. "I think Kyle Flores needs to get down here to look at him. In my medical opinion, we can't wait until Monday."

"I'll call Kyle and be right down." Without saying anything more, Aaron ended the call.

Reassured that Aaron was doing his part, she sank into the chair at Joey's bedside. She hadn't brought her stethoscope to the conference but wished she had it now so she could listen to the little boy's heart and lungs. Since she couldn't do that herself, she pressed the call button to summon the nurse.

"Maggie?" Aaron entered the room, his expression full of concern. He'd gotten down there quicker than she'd expected. "Kyle's on his way. His previous case took longer than he'd expected."

"Good." She pressed the call button for the nurse, stood, and crossed over to join him. "What do you think? Will Kyle take him to the OR?"

"I'm not sure." He surprised her by wrapping his arm around her shoulder. "We'll do our best to talk him into it."

That made her smile. "Works for me."

Rachel hurried into the room. "Is there a problem?"

"I'd like a full set of vitals," Maggie explained. "I'm concerned Joey is running a fever."

"Of course." Rachel appeared flustered but quickly went to work. Joey didn't appreciate being woken up and began to whine again about his tummy hurting.

"It's okay. I'm here." She bent over the little boy,

smoothing his dark hair from his forehead. His skin felt warmer now, and she glanced at Aaron in concern. "I hope Kyle gets here soon."

"He will." Aaron came over to stand beside her. Rachel removed the stethoscope from her ears, glancing at the two of them. "His blood pressure is much lower than it was before, and his pulse is higher."

"Double-check his temperature," Maggie said.

Rachel did so, then turned so they could read the screen for themselves. Joey's fever was now 101.6 degrees Fahrenheit.

Not her imagination. She exchanged a concerned glance with Aaron as Rachel entered the readings into the computer.

She was about to ask Aaron to call his colleague again when Kyle hurried into the room. He glanced from Joey to her and Aaron and finally addressed Rachel. "What's going on? What's changed?"

"His vitals are not good," Rachel admitted. "He's running a fever, and his blood pressure has dropped. He's running tachycardic, too, likely because of the fever."

"Let me borrow your stethoscope," Kyle said to Rachel. When she handed it over, Kyle bent over Joey to listen to his heart and lungs. When he finished, Kyle handed the stethoscope back and addressed Aaron. "Have we gotten in touch with his parent or guardian?"

"No," Maggie said. "The police and I questioned Joey. He says he doesn't have a father or aunts and uncles." She glanced at Aaron. "It sounds like the hospital administrators have reached out to legal counsel, but it may be too late in the day to get an emergency guardian hearing in front of a judge."

"I tried," Aaron said. "They were sympathetic but determined to go through proper channels."

Kyle blew out an exasperated sigh. "His condition is growing tenuous. But I cannot honestly say he's on the verge of dying."

"Hospital policy considers a procedure emergent if there is a high likelihood of loss of life or limb within twenty-four hours," Aaron said. "Do you really think Joey's condition will improve?"

"I didn't say that," Kyle argued, his tone testy. Then he sighed again. "Okay, okay. I can't be responsible for risking this child's life. I'll document that the procedure is emergent, and we'll get him ready to go to the OR."

"Thank you," Maggie said. "I know you're in a difficult position, but I appreciate your willingness to take the risk."

"Yeah, well, better to risk getting yelled at or sued rather than losing a child's life," Kyle muttered. He turned toward Rachel. "I need you to place an IV and start maintenance fluids. I'll write the orders," he added when she looked as if she might argue.

"Of course." Rachel hurried off to gather the supplies, leaving Kyle to enter the orders into the computer.

"What can I do to help?" Aaron asked. "Would you like me to call up to the OR?"

"Yeah, sure. Let them know the three o'clock patient is going forward as scheduled," Kyle said as he typed on the keyboard. "I had him listed as tentative, pending the outcome of his scans."

Maggie knew the scan itself wasn't the reason they were moving forward with the procedure, but rather the abrupt change in Joey's condition. Sepsis, which is caused by an infection that enters the blood stream, could be deadly.

And the problem with kids was that they tended to compensate for their illness but then abruptly crash.

She couldn't bear for that to happen with Joey.

Aaron stepped to the side to make his calls to the OR while Rachel and Kyle discussed treatment options for Joey. She was glad to hear Kyle wanted the child to get his first dose of antibiotics prior to the procedure.

"I'll put a rush on that," Rachel said.

"Thanks." Kyle glanced at her. "I'm sorry, I don't think we've met."

"Dr. Maggie Dall, anesthesiologist." She shook his hand.

"Nice to meet you," Kyle said with a tired smile. "If you don't mind my asking, if you're not Joey's guardian, why are you here?"

She flushed. "I responded to the bus accident with Aaron. I...we..." She faltered, then said, "We used to be married. Anyway, Joey latched onto me in the bus, so I've stayed with him."

Kyle's eyebrows shot up in surprise, but he didn't have time to respond as Aaron stepped forward. "Everything is all set. The OR team is getting room eight ready for Joey's emergency abdominal exploration procedure."

"Great." Kyle checked his watch. "As soon as the IV is placed and the antibiotics are infusing, we can move."

Rachel returned with the supplies. Maggie was impressed she had gotten the antibiotics rushed up from the pharmacy. She held Joey as Rachel started the IV; his crying made her heart hurt.

"There now, the poke is over," she said, as Rachel secured the IV in place. "You'll feel better soon."

"I want my mommy," Joey said between sniffles.

"I know you do." She kept him close to her side. "Don't worry, I'll stay with you."

He nodded, resting his head against her chest. His little body was warm to the touch, radiating heat. She glanced over to see Kyle and Aaron talking in low voices.

"Okay, we'll head up to the OR now," Kyle finally said, after they were finished. "Maggie, do you want to walk along with us?"

"Yes." She tried to slip away from Joey, but he clung to her much the way he had on the bus, as if he were deathly afraid to let her go. "Actually, I'll carry him."

Kyle looked at Aaron who shrugged. Then he nodded. "Rachel, will you push the IV pole as we go?"

"Ah, sure." From the shocked expression on Rachel's face, Maggie assumed carrying a child to the OR wasn't normal practice.

She didn't care. She cradled Joey close while following Kyle through the hallways to the OR suites. When the anesthesiologist met up with them, she continued to hold Joey while he was given medication to put him to sleep. Only once the little boy was completely relaxed and asleep did she allow the medical team to place the child on the OR table.

Forcing herself to back away wasn't easy. As the medical professionals surrounded the little boy, she asked God to heal Joey.

And to guide Kyle's skilled hands as he performed surgery.

CHAPTER FOUR

Walking back to the emergency department, Aaron glanced at Maggie. She had been unusually quiet after leaving Joey with the OR team. They'd managed to get over the hurdle of consent, but the little boy's future was still in limbo.

With his mother gone and no other family members having been identified, it was likely Joey would end up in the foster care system. The situation was reminiscent of what his brother Adam and his wife, Krista, had gone through when a safe haven baby had been dropped off at Adam's pediatric clinic.

"I assume Joey will be admitted to a regular room after his surgery?" Maggie asked, breaking the silence.

"Yes." They'd reached the emergency department. She went into Joey's room to grab her bag. "Would you like me to find out which room he'll be in?"

"Please." She managed a smile. "I'd like to wait in his room."

"You're sticking around?" He shouldn't have been surprised after the way Maggie had clearly bonded with the child. "I assumed you had a flight back to Boston later tonight."

"I do, but I'm not heading back yet." She frowned, reaching into her bag for her phone. "I need to formally check out of the hotel, then contact the airline about changing my flight. I'm not due back to work until Monday, but I'll ask my colleagues to cover for me a few more days."

"I see." Adam was tempted to offer her the chance to stay at his place but managed to hold back. First of all, being thrown together by chance didn't mean a reconciliation was in their future. They'd both moved on, leaving a chasm of hurt feelings and, yeah, even some bitterness behind. But he knew Maggie well enough to know she was not going to leave Joey until she knew things were settled.

The only problem being that could take time. The last thing he wanted was to have Maggie invading his personal space for the next few days. Maybe even stretching into a full week.

"There must be a hotel close to the hospital," she said as if reading his mind.

"There is. It's within walking distance." He hesitated, then said, "I can give you a ride back to the hotel. Do you have a rental car?"

"No, but I'll get a rideshare." She didn't look too concerned. "I don't want to trouble you any more than I already have. If you could please just tell me which room they'll admit Joey into, that would be great. I can handle the rest myself."

"Okay." Maggie always had been fiercely independent. "But I am not on duty today, so why don't you let me drive you back to the Pfister? I'll call my brother Adam on the way. His wife, Krista, went through the process of being a foster parent. She might have some insight regarding Joey's future."

"Really?" The news piqued her interest. "I didn't realize Adam was married."

"All the sibs are married now, except for Andrea. She... lost her husband, Stuart, four months ago in a car crash while he was traveling." He hated knowing he was the only one who'd failed at marriage.

"Oh, I'm so sorry to hear that. I'm sure it's been difficult for Andrea and her two kids to cope."

"Yes, the family has rallied around her, but it's been hard." He gestured for her to come with him. "I'm parked in the physicians parking lot."

After a moment's hesitation, she fell into step beside him. It had been one thing to be together while taking care of crash victims on the bus and dealing with Joey's medical care. But now it was just the two of them.

Alone together in a way they hadn't been in over two years.

"Are you sure about sticking around?" he asked as they approached his vehicle. "I can keep an eye on Joey's progress."

"I'm sure." She gave him a nod when he opened her car door for her. "I'm the one he's been clinging to since the accident. I won't abandon him."

He nodded, then closed her door. There was no denying the little boy had latched onto Maggie. But it wasn't like she could just step in and take the boy into her home.

Could she?

It burned a little to know that she was probably considering her options regarding adopting Joey. Yet when he'd suggested they adopt a baby, she'd stared at him as if he were crazy and walked away.

Two years since their divorce and he still resented her for that.

He really needed to get over it. To forgive her, the way God would want him to. He'd fallen away from God during his time in Boston, but now that he'd returned home, he'd begun attending church again.

Maybe that was part of the reason things hadn't worked out for him and Maggie. They'd let their respective careers get in the way.

Shaking off the useless regrets, he used his hands-free function to call Adam. His brother didn't answer, likely he was with a patient, so he left a message. "Hey, call me back when you have a minute. I have a few questions for you and Krista about the foster care system. Thanks." He hit the end button.

"Why would Adam and Krista have firsthand knowledge of the foster care system?" Maggie asked.

"Last Christmas, a safe haven baby was left in Adam's pediatric clinic. Krista had hoped to adopt Joy, but my brother Alec helped find the infant's mother." He shrugged. "Joy was reunited with her mother, which proved to be a happy ending for everyone involved."

"I see. So this is your way of warning me not to get too attached to Joey because his family will likely be found." There was a hint of annoyance in her tone.

"Maggie, you must know that you can't just step in and adopt a kid on the spot." He let his own frustration show. "Nothing is that easy. Just because the police haven't found Joey's family yet doesn't mean there isn't someone out there who will love and care for him."

She turned away to stare out the window. Then she

sighed. "I know that. It's just..." She let her voice trail off. Then she said, "Joey needs me, especially now that he's undergoing surgery. I won't leave him alone. I'll be ecstatic if Joey experiences the same happy ending baby Joy did."

Would she? He wasn't convinced. But he decided to let it go.

The drive back to the Pfister didn't take long. Shifting into park, he glanced at her. "Would you like me to help? Or wait here?"

"Wait here. It won't take me long." She jumped out of the car and slammed her door shut before he could say anything more.

Why was he prolonging the agony? He could text her the information from Adam and Krista, along with Joey's room number. He didn't have to play the role of her rideshare driver.

His phone rang. Seeing Adam's name on the screen, he quickly answered. "Sorry to bother you at work, Adam."

"No problem, just saw my last patient of the day," Adam said cheerfully. "I'm heading to the hospital to make rounds. Why the need to know about the foster care system?"

He quickly filled his brother in on the bus crash and Maggie's attachment to Joey Johnson. "Last we heard, no family members have been found."

"Maggie is here with you?" Trust his brother to zero in on the biggest sore spot. "Like you're together?"

"No, we're not together," he swiftly responded. "We just happened to be standing outside the Pfister when the crash happened. She was at the medical conference too."

"The one where you were presenting?" Adam asked. "Maybe Maggie specifically chose that conference to reconnect with you."

"No, she didn't. Can we please focus on the issue at hand?" He glanced out the window, relieved Maggie wasn't back yet. "Joey is having surgery, and it looks like he'll end up in foster care."

"That is exactly what will happen if they don't find any family members," Adam agreed. "Krista is still a foster parent, although she hasn't taken in any kids yet. I can ask her if she's open to taking Joey in."

"Well, I'm not sure that's necessary." Maggie emerged from the hotel and was heading his way with a small roll-away suitcase in tow. "How long did the process take?"

"Several weeks, although Joy had specific medical needs that helped speed things up. Not unlike Joey, if he's having surgery. Medical professionals have the advantage when it comes to fostering kids with medical needs."

"Great, that information is really helpful. I have to go. I'll be in touch later." Adam quickly ended the call, then opened the trunk. Sliding out from behind the wheel, he rushed over to take her bag. "Here, let me."

"Who were you talking to?" Maggie asked, as she allowed him to place her small suitcase in the trunk.

Figures she'd seen him on the phone. He sighed, closed the trunk, and turned to face her. "Adam. He's on his way to Children's Memorial. I'll fill you in along the way."

"Great, thanks." She grabbed the passenger door handle. "I can't wait to hear what he said."

Yeah, somehow he had a feeling Maggie would try to become a foster parent to Joey. Yet rather than being happy, he battled a wave of anger.

Apparently, Maggie was more than happy to go down the path of adopting a child, as long as she wasn't married to him.

TENSION SHIMMERED off Aaron as he drove her toward the hotel located within walking distance of Children's Memorial Hospital. Maggie was just as eager to put distance between them. The moment he pulled up the drive to park in front of the double doors leading to the lobby, she jumped out of the car.

"Thanks for the ride. I'll find out about Joey's room when I get back to the hospital. Take care." She hoped her smile didn't look as forced as it felt.

"I'll give you a ride," he offered.

"No thanks. You said walking distance. And that works out well for me." She slammed her door, went around to grab her suitcase from the back, then hurried inside.

She really should have insisted on taking a rideshare, she thought as she smiled at the hotel clerk. She didn't have to talk to Aaron's brother to find out about the foster care process. She was confident the social worker would have all the information she needed.

"Three days?" the clerk asked.

"Yes, please. It may be longer, depending on how things go," she said.

"I understand." The woman's gaze was sympathetic, making Maggie realize that many people stayed here to be near their sick loved ones. "Extending your stay won't be a problem."

"Thank you." Maggie tucked her credit card back into her bag, grabbed the room key, and turned away. Her intent was to dump her suitcase in her room and head directly back to the hospital.

Yet she needed to slow down, to make the proper

arrangements with Johns Hopkins. Other patients depended on her too. As did her colleagues.

Joey would be in surgery for at least an hour, likely longer. Then he'd spent time in the post-anesthesia care unit for another hour. She could probably convince Kyle to let her see Joey in the PACU, but there was no reason to rush back to Children's Memorial. She needed to take a few minutes to adapt her travel plans.

Her stomach growled with hunger as she dealt with the airline and her boss at Hopkins. She changed into a comfortable pair of jeans and a sweater, the clothes she'd planned to wear home on the plane and headed outside. She'd grab a bite to eat in the cafeteria, then find Joey's room number.

Was she crazy to rearrange her life for the little boy? Just remembering how he clung to her made her heart ache. No, she wasn't crazy. That child needed her.

And if she were honest, she'd admit she needed him too.

The two years since leaving Aaron had been more difficult than she could have imagined. Initially, she'd thrown herself into her work, taking on additional call shifts for trauma cases just to prolong the moment she returned to her empty condo. Then she'd tried to get back out there, but after two disastrous dates, she realized she wasn't ready. It didn't help that every man she met wasn't nearly as attractive as Aaron. Or as accomplished as Aaron.

Or as sweet as Aaron.

Giving up on a social life, she'd gone back to concentrating on her professional life. But even that hadn't helped. Her days were nothing but work, eat, sleep, and work again. Even the job she normally loved didn't seem important anymore.

She'd wanted to have a baby so badly. Accepting that wasn't an option for her had not been easy.

Now there was a motherless little boy that needed her support. She quickened her pace to reach the hospital. After entering the building, she was able to find the cafeteria easily enough.

And abruptly stopped when she saw Aaron seated at a table. He was alone, his gaze locking on hers.

Why hadn't she considered he'd be in here eating a late lunch or early dinner too? Swallowing a groan, she gave him a nod as she headed over to see what looked good.

After paying for her grilled chicken and fries, she saw Aaron waving her over. Hiding a grimace, she crossed over to join him.

"Joey is doing well," he said by way of greeting. "Kyle has drained the hematoma and is doing a washout of his abdomen now. The antibiotics appear to be working."

"That's great news," she said, munching on a french fry. "How long before he hits the PACU?"

"Thirty minutes, give or take a few." Aaron looked down at his phone. "Joey's been admitted to room 721 on seven south, that's generally where kids his age are cared for."

She made a mental note of the room number as she picked up her grilled chicken sandwich. "You didn't have to stay here for me. I know my way around a hospital."

He shrugged. "I missed lunch too."

Had he chosen to eat in the cafeteria hoping to see her? And why was he being so nice and supportive now?

Honestly, she would have preferred eating alone.

Reminding herself that Aaron had gone out of his way to get an update on Joey and to get his room number, she told herself to relax. "I was thinking of calling Officer

Thomas to see if he has found any of Joey's family members yet."

"I figure the social worker will be all over that," he said. "Here, I meant to give you Kyle's phone number so that you have it." After he pressed a few keys on his phone screen, her phone dinged with an incoming text.

"Great." She added Kyle Flores's name and number to her contact list. "I won't abuse the privilege."

"I know you won't." Aaron waved that off. "I should tell you that I spoke to Adam. He mentioned his wife, Krista, is still registered as a foster parent." Aaron caught her gaze. "I can ask if Krista would consider taking Joey in on a temporary basis. Child Protective Services is more likely to place Joey with a medical professional to help him recover from surgery."

"I was thinking of taking Joey in." The words popped out of her mouth before she could stop them. "I mean, I know I'd have to go through the process of becoming a foster parent, but that shouldn't be too difficult."

Aaron sat back in his seat. "I had a feeling you were going to say that."

She took another bite of her sandwich, even though her appetite was fading fast. They were treading on dangerous ground. It had been a long day that wasn't close to being over, and she wasn't in the mood to rehash their past arguments.

"Look, Aaron, I appreciate everything you've done regarding Joey's care. But I didn't come here to discuss what went wrong in our marriage. I'd like to stay focused on taking care of Joey. I think it's best if you get back to your job too. I'm not sure exactly what your role is here in the hospital, but you must have patients to see."

He arched a brow. "Yeah, I kinda got the hint when you

bolted out of my car when I pulled up to the hotel. Keep in mind, you came to the conference here in Milwaukee, not the other way around."

"Yet you're the one who followed me outside where we happened to witness the bus crash," she shot back. Then she winced upon realizing they were beginning to sound like a pair of five-year-olds. She held up a hand. "Please, Aaron, I don't want to argue. Let's just move on from this unexpected reunion, okay?"

There was a long pause before he finally nodded. "Yeah. Sure."

"Thank you." She finished the last of her chicken sandwich, then rose to her feet. "Take care of yourself."

"You too." To his credit, he didn't stand or try to follow as she left the cafeteria. Rather than heading back to the lobby, she took the elevators to the seventh floor. Parents were usually allowed to wait in their child's room while the patient was undergoing a procedure. Since Joey's mother couldn't be there, Maggie went up to the main nurse's station to let the nurse assigned to Joey's room know she was there for the little boy.

"I thought Joey Johnson lost his mother." Nurse Clarice frowned.

"He did. I happened to respond to the bus accident, and he latched onto me while we tried to resuscitate his mother. I need you to trust me on this. Joey will be more relaxed after surgery when he sees me."

"Okay." Clarice did not look convinced. Maggie hoped she wouldn't run into this reluctance with every nurse on the unit.

"Please let the PACU know that I'm waiting here and that I'd like to see Joey as soon as possible." She'd used her best authoritarian tone but then softened. "I really don't want that poor little boy to wake up in a room full of strangers all alone."

That seemed to do the trick. Clarice nodded. "You're right, that would be awful. I'll gladly let them know."

Maggie smiled and hovered nearby as Clarice made the call. A moment later, Clarice hung up the phone. "Joey is on his way to the PACU now, and Dr. Kyle said you can head up there. Do you know where it is?"

"No, but I'm sure I can find it. Which floor?"

"The OR suites are all on the third floor. The PACU is to the south, like directly beneath us."

"Great, thanks again." Maggie quickly turned and headed back to the elevators. The third floor looked similar to the operating room setup at Johns Hopkins. Or maybe most ORs looked the same. If not for the different shade of blue scrubs, she would have felt she was back in Boston.

The doors to the PACU opened when she stepped forward. She frowned when she saw Aaron standing and talking with Kyle. Why was he here? Then a horrible thought hit, and she quickly rushed over to join them. "What happened? Is Joey okay?"

"His condition is stable," Kyle said with a tired smile. "But he's not out of the woods yet. His fever has not come all the way down, so I decided to keep a drain in his abdomen in case he needs to have another irrigation with antibiotic solution."

That wasn't entirely unexpected, so she nodded. "But he's otherwise stable. He hadn't needed any blood products or anything, right?"

"Correct," Kyle affirmed. "He's in bay number three. You can go over and see him for yourself."

With a nod, she turned and walked to the third bay. This area didn't have individual rooms like the rest of the hospital. There were only curtains separating one patient from the other, mostly so the hospital staff could reach their patients quickly if needed.

Anesthesiologists cared for patients while they were in the PACU. Only once the anesthesiologist signed off did the surgeon take over.

Bending over Joey's bedside, it felt strange to be there as a patient visitor rather than the doc in charge. Her gaze automatically went to the monitor where his vitals were displayed on the screen, then she checked the IV solution. She couldn't fault the care Kyle and the anesthesiologist provided.

"Joey? Can you hear me?" She gently took his hand. He was still groggy from the meds and the anesthesia, but his fingers closed around hers in a tight grip.

Yes, this was where she belonged. And if she had her way, she wouldn't be leaving Joey's bedside anytime soon.

CHAPTER FIVE

Aaron hovered in the PACU until Joey was discharged from the care of the anesthesiologist. Maggie remained at the boy's bedside, doing an admirable job of staying out of the way.

He'd noticed how she'd kept an eye on the little boy's vital signs, encouraging him to breathe if his oxygenation level dropped too low. She appeared stressed when he cried out in pain, and he knew she wanted nothing more than to help the child feel better.

It was tempting to head up to Joey's room, but there was no good excuse for him to show up there. He'd done his part, getting Kyle involved so he could do the procedure, calling the police to check if they'd found any family for the child, and helping Maggie get settled in the hotel nearby. A hotel she wouldn't use as he felt certain she'd spend the night in Joey's room.

No, the only reason to head up to the seventh floor now was to see Maggie again. Talk about being a glutton for punishment. He should be over her by now, two years after their divorce.

He wasn't.

His problem, not hers. He forced himself to head home, even though there was nothing remotely appealing about the empty house he'd purchased upon his return to Milwaukee.

Watching Maggie and Joey made him keenly aware of what he'd lost. He'd tried to move on, to find the family he'd always wanted, but he hadn't met anyone like Maggie.

Pathetic the only woman he wanted was the one who'd left him.

The ringing of his phone dragged him from sleep, a dream in which he and Maggie had decided to get back together. Too bad it was only a dream. He rubbed his eyes, noting the time was three in the morning. The number on the screen was from Children's Memorial. He wasn't on call, but that didn't always matter.

"This is Aaron Monroe," he said in a voice husky with sleep.

"Dr. Monroe, I'm sorry to bother you, but we have a baby girl who's been admitted with what I believe is a congenital heart defect." The resident on the other end of the line sounded a bit nervous, as if he knew he was taking a risk in calling the chairman of the department in the middle of the night. "I'm calling you directly because the surgeon on call hadn't answered his calls or pages."

All sleepiness faded as Aaron digested that news. He already knew who was on call—Dr. Dale Fullerton—and this was not the first time the guy hadn't responded to calls or pages.

"I can try again," the resident said. "But someone needs to see this little girl ASAP."

"Don't bother with Fullerton, I'm on my way." Aaron rolled off the bed. "I'm less than fifteen minutes out."

"I...didn't give you a name. How did you know the doc who didn't respond was Fullerton?" the resident asked.

He winced, realizing he shouldn't have filled in the name of the attending who was supposed to be on call. The guy's inability to respond to his calls was Aaron's problem to tackle as the chairman of the department. It wasn't the resident's concern. "What's the name and room number of our patient?"

"Grace Baxter, she's on six south," the resident replied.

"Great. I'll be there soon."

"Thank you."

Aaron threw on casual clothes, brushed his teeth, then headed out the door. The home he'd purchased was close to the hospital, so he made it within the allotted timeframe. Using his ID badge to access the locked doors, he strode toward the elevators. He wondered how Maggie and Joey were doing, but there wasn't time for a detour to the seventh floor.

He found Grace Baxter easily enough, and a quick assessment with the resident, Jamal Cook, confirmed the resident's diagnosis that Grace was suffering from a patent foramen ovale, which was the formal term for having a hole between two chambers of the heart. What concerned him was the way the little girl was breathing too fast and the dusky blueish tint around her lips. He didn't think this could wait until Monday; he'd prefer to operate right away to prevent complications.

He turned to Jamal. "I need you to call the OR to get a room set up for her ASAP. Good call on escalating this to the attending level."

"I—thanks." Jamal Cook flushed with gratitude, then hurried off to make the arrangements.

Aaron turned his attention to Grace's mother who

looked horrified by the news that her daughter needed surgery to correct a hole in her heart.

"I don't understand," the woman said, wringing her hands. "How did this happen?"

He needed to choose his words carefully. He didn't want to throw another physician under the bus, but Grace was six months old, and he was convinced she was born with the cardiac condition. One that had been missed by her pediatrician and the hospital staff who'd tended to the baby after her birth. It wasn't always easy to determine a patent foramen ovale, but the way the child's symptoms were presenting, he suspected someone should have noticed.

"Babies can have heart conditions that are present at birth but that aren't diagnosed right away. Babies pretty much eat and sleep, so there's not as much stress on the heart until they get older. You didn't do anything wrong," he hastened to reassure the mother. "The hole in Grace's heart should have closed on its own after her birth. But it didn't. I know this sounds scary, but I want to assure you that I've done this procedure hundreds of times."

The exhausted mother brushed away her tears. "If you say so, Doctor. I want Grace to feel better."

"She'll do very well after the procedure. I'll need you to sign a surgical consent form," he went on. "There are risks to every procedure, but we do everything possible to minimize those risks."

Jamal returned with the paper consent form. Aaron explained the procedure at length using terms he hoped Grace's mother could understand. Once she signed off on the consent, he rested a hand on the woman's arm.

"I'll take good care of Grace," he assured her.

"Thank you, Dr. Monroe." She sniffled and turned her attention back to her baby girl.

Leaving Grace and her mother with Jamal, who would get the little girl prepped for the procedure, he headed to the locker room to change into scrubs. He was wide awake now, and as he scrubbed his hands and forearms at the deep sink, his thoughts turned to Maggie and Joey. Behind him, the OR staff who had been called in on this early Saturday were scurrying around to ready the room.

He told himself they were likely doing fine. He and Maggie might be divorced, but if she thought Joey needed something urgently, she wouldn't hesitate to call.

Time to focus on Grace's upcoming procedure. Even though it was a relatively routine case for pediatric cardiac surgeons, he'd learned early in his career to never take a case for granted. Anything could go wrong, especially when dealing with young babies who didn't have much in the way of a medical history.

Allergies to drugs and anesthetics were not uncommon. He'd come to appreciate the talent and skills of the anesthesiologists on staff here at Children's Memorial, but they weren't Maggie.

Then again, he hadn't worked with Maggie since their split. She'd moved into working with trauma patients, much like Joey.

Forcing thoughts of Maggie out of his head, he dried his hands and donned his protective gear. For the next few hours, his primary concern would be Grace Baxter. He might have failed at his marriage, but he was still a good surgeon.

All he cared about was making sure Grace came through this open-heart procedure without difficulty.

MAGGIE AWOKE for what seemed to be the tenth time to Joey crying out in pain. As soon as the pain medication wore off, he became restless and upset.

She didn't blame him. Hitting the call light to summon the nurse, she stretched out on the bed beside the little boy. "It's okay. I'm here. You're going to be okay."

"My tummy hurts," he whimpered.

"I know, sweetie. I know." Spending the night with Joey gave her a new appreciation for parents with sick children. Not only was it nearly impossible to get any sleep, but the overwhelming sense of helplessness was just as difficult to overcome. There was no getting around the fact that surgery hurt. She would have given anything to be able to ease Joey's suffering.

The little boy rested against her until the night-shift nurse brought his pain medication. He'd stopped asking about his mother, which was a blessing. Every time she tried to describe how his mother was in heaven watching over him, tears filled her eyes.

At seven in the morning, Kyle Flores came in to see them. He didn't look surprised to find her there as he nodded in greeting. "How is my star patient this morning?"

"His vitals are stable," Maggie said, as Joey rested against her. His eyelids drooped as the pain meds had kicked in. "He's been crying out in pain every four hours between doses."

Kyle pulled out his stethoscope as he approached the bed. "As you well know, this will be the worst day. The pain should lessen over the next twenty-four hours."

She did know, but that didn't make it any easier to watch the little boy suffer. She held Joey as Kyle listened to his heart and lungs. The boy barely moved, having grown accustomed to the hospital staff using stethoscopes to examine him.

"I'm reassured he's not running a fever," Kyle said when he finished. "How much blood is coming from the drain?"

"Less than ten cc's all night," she said.

"Good. If that continues, I can remove the drain later this afternoon." Kyle eyed her thoughtfully. "No news yet on a guardian?"

She shook her head. "I'm hoping maybe we'll hear something today."

"Yeah." He regarded her thoughtfully. "I take it you and Aaron are close. You mentioned you used to be married."

"Uh, yes. I—we worked together at Johns Hopkins." She saw no reason to explain about their divorce. "I learned Aaron was anxious to return to Milwaukee to be closer to his family."

"Yeah, well, being offered the chairmanship over the entire pediatric cardiac surgery department is another good reason to relocate," Kyle said with a wry smile. "He's the youngest surgeon to be in that position in the history of the Milwaukee Medical Center."

Chairman of Pediatric Cardiac Surgery? She hadn't realized Aaron was that much of a bigwig. Children's Memorial may not have the same prestige as Johns Hopkins, but being the chairman of an entire department was impressive. No wonder surgeons like Kyle had jumped to do his bidding. "Yes, he's a talented guy."

"True." Kyle crossed over to log into the computer. He scrolled through the data, made a few notes, then turned back to face her. "Do you need anything else?"

"No thanks." She appreciated his treating her like a colleague. "Will you be in to remove the drain or one of the residents?" It was a Saturday, so she fully expected Kyle would delegate the procedure.

He hesitated, then shrugged. "I'll stop by later and take care of it myself."

She hadn't meant to pressure him into coming back in but nodded gratefully. Maybe she was being overprotective, but she wanted the best for Joey.

The little boy didn't need to suffer any complications from his procedure.

"Thanks again, Kyle." She rested back against the pillow after the trauma surgeon left. She was getting hungry but didn't want to eat in front of the little boy. Not that Joey had complained about feeling hungry.

Joey fell asleep against her, his breathing deep and regular. She'd made a game out of using his deep breathing machine, and even though it hurt for him to take deep breaths, he seemed to like the challenge of raising the ball in the plastic container.

Glancing at her watch, she debated slipping away to grab a bite to eat. Joey wouldn't miss her while he was sleeping, and based on previous medication doses, he'd be down for the count for at least two hours.

Pressing a kiss to the top of his head, she gently eased away. Joey shifted on the bed but relaxed against the pillow. She tucked the stuffed dalmatian dog she'd picked up at the gift shop next to him.

For a long moment, she watched him sleep, then shoved her feet into her shoes and ran her fingers through her long curly hair.

Breakfast and coffee, not necessarily in that order, she thought wryly as she slipped from the room.

She was waiting for the elevator to arrive when Aaron emerged from the stairwell. He stopped abruptly, clearly not expecting to see her. He looked good, despite his wrinkled scrubs, dangling face mask, and his dark hair tousled from this surgical cap.

"Are you coming from the OR?" she asked.

"Yeah." He rubbed the back of his neck. "Spent the past three hours repairing a patent foraman ovale."

"I didn't realize you were on call last night."

"I wasn't. But you know how that goes." He glanced down the hall toward Joey's room. "How's Joey this morning?"

"Doing well. You just missed Kyle. He's already been in making rounds." The ding of the elevator startled her. "I was heading down to grab breakfast."

"Great, I'm starved."

She hadn't intended to issue an invitation, but there was no way to gracefully refuse Aaron's intent to accompany her to the cafeteria. She stepped into the elevator, then held the door for him.

They rode in silence down to the cafeteria. She blamed her lack of sleep for being unable to think of anything to say. Then she remembered his patient. "How did the surgery go?"

"Fine. Grace is doing well." He waited for her to exit the elevator first. "She's in good hands with the anesthesiologist and nursing staff in the PACU."

She nodded, trying to come up with another topic of conversation. Anything other than their personal relationship.

Thankfully, the cafeteria was busy that morning, and the chattering staff members grabbing food made it difficult to talk. Since they'd eaten breakfast together hundreds of times, they crossed over to the grill for eggs, bacon, and toast.

Ten minutes later, they were seated at a quiet table in the corner of the room. "So, tell me why you had to come in to operate last night?" Maggie had decided that the best thing was to talk about work. It was the one area where they'd been the most compatible.

Until the demands of their careers had driven another wedge between them.

"Most of the surgeons here are great," Aaron said, taking a bite of bacon. "But there's one guy in particular who often claims he didn't hear his phone or his pager when he's on call."

Her eyes widened. "That's not good."

"No, it's not. I'll have to bring him in for a chat." Aaron grimaced. "I don't mind being in a leadership position for the most part, handling more paperwork and attending meetings are fine. But this kind of thing?" He frowned. "Makes me feel like I'm dealing with a bunch of idiotic teenagers sometimes."

She couldn't help but laugh. There was no shortage of drama within the medical profession, much like any other environment. "That's why you get paid the big bucks," she teased.

"Yeah, well, it seemed like a good idea at the time," he groused. They ate in silence for a few minutes. Then he reached for his coffee. "I've been up since three in the morning. How did Joey sleep?"

"He woke up every few hours in pain." She took a bite of toast. "He's been really good about not touching the drain site, though. And he's not running a fever anymore either. He has minimal drainage from the tube, and if that continues, Kyle plans to remove it. I think he's well on the road to recovery."

"I'm glad to hear that." Aaron held her gaze for a long

moment, and she could practically see the questions spinning in his mind. She looked away, not wanting to get into a heavy discussion about why she'd stayed overnight in Joey's room.

Or the steps she would have to take to become the boy's guardian if there were no family members to be found.

The latter wasn't likely. Over the nighttime hours she'd spent in his room, she'd steeled herself for the inevitable. Joey's mother had parents or siblings. Someone would step forward to care for the little boy.

But if they didn't? It was hard not to let the hope build in her heart.

Before she could try to change the subject, his phone beeped. He pulled out the device and glanced at the message. "Grace is doing well. They just removed her breathing tube."

"That's wonderful." She had to give him credit where it was due. Aaron was an excellent surgeon. One of the best she'd worked with. "I'm sure the little girl's mother will be relieved she's going to make a full recovery."

He nodded, and they ate for a while in silence. She quickly finished the rest of her meal, anxious to bring an end to the awkwardness between them. "I need to get back upstairs before Joey's pain meds wear off. I don't want him to wake up alone."

"Maggie." He grabbed her wrist as she stood to leave. "I know it's probably too late, but you shouldn't get too emotionally attached to him. I don't want to see you get hurt."

She bit back the urge to snap at him. "I don't care if I get hurt. That little boy has just lost his mother. He needs me to be there for him."

"I know that, but..."

"But nothing," she interrupted, tugging her wrist free. "I understand he may have family members out there. If so, that's fine. I still intend to be there to help Joey transition to his new caregivers. The fact that he doesn't know anything about a father or aunts, uncles, or grandparents isn't a good sign. Even if he has relatives, they will be strangers to him."

"Yes, that's true," Aaron murmured. "I understand your attachment to him."

Did he? She wasn't so sure. She managed a reassuring smile and picked up her tray. "Take care of yourself. And little Grace." Without waiting for him to respond, she dropped her tray of dirty dishes on the conveyor belt that would carry them around back to the dishwasher, then headed out of the cafeteria. She remembered passing a coffee shop in the lobby, so she headed there for a quick refill before taking the elevator back up to the seventh floor.

Sipping her coffee, she poked her head into Joey's room. He was still sleeping, so she walked down to the small lounge located at the end of the hall.

She imagined this space was used for smaller patient and family gatherings, but it was empty now. Tired of sitting, she stood off to the side, absently watching some cartoon show on the television. Disney+ was a big hit here.

Smiling, she remembered how Joey had loved watching the television in his room. She didn't know much about Joey's mother's financial situation, but from what she could tell, Joey hadn't been exposed to many Disney or other animated movies. It was a good way to distract him from the pain.

After finishing her coffee, she headed back down the hall to Joey's room. And stopped abruptly when she saw a familiar police officer walking toward her. Officer Thomas wasn't alone; he had a skinny tattooed man with him. The guy's pale and sunken features along with the ratty and stained long-sleeved shirt he wore with equally stained and holey jeans did not portray a man of confidence. Quite the opposite. She wished she could see his arms because his twitchy movements and shifty glances from side to side made her think he might be a drug addict.

A sense of dread washed over her. *Please, Lord, not this man. Please don't let this man be Joey's father.*

But based on the grim expression on Officer Thomas's face, he was.

CHAPTER SIX

After dawdling over his coffee and fighting a wave of despair over his broken relationship with Maggie, Aaron had left the cafeteria, intending to head up to the PACU to check on Grace. Granted, Jamal would have let him know if something was amiss, but the idea of heading home didn't hold much appeal.

As pathetic as it sounded, he had to force himself not to go up to Joey's room to see Maggie. And to check on the child's progress.

When he ran into a police officer standing near a skinny, disheveled man at the elevator, he slowed his pace. A quick glance at the officer's uniform confirmed the cop's last name was Thomas. He frowned, thinking back over the events of yesterday. Hadn't Maggie mentioned an Officer Thomas coming in to interview her and Joey? He hung back, waiting for the cop and skinny guy to get into the elevator first. When Officer Thomas pushed the button for the seventh floor, a sick feeling settled in his gut.

Was this Joey's father?

Rather than pressing the button for the third floor

where the PACU was located, Aaron rode with the pair to the seventh floor, hoping and praying he was wrong.

While instinctively knowing he wasn't.

Officer Thomas and the skinny, disheveled man left the elevator first. He let them get several steps ahead of him in case he was wrong. Looking over the skinny guy's shoulder, he saw Maggie striding purposefully toward them with a stern expression etched on her features. When she stopped, blocking the doorway to Joey's room, he almost smiled.

"Officer Thomas." Maggie's voice was ice. "What brings you here this morning?"

"Dr. Dall." The officer gave her a nod. "This is Oliver Chism. He is listed as Joseph Johnson's father on his birth certificate."

"I see." Maggie crossed her arms over her chest and gave the skinny guy a piercing look. "Does that mean he's been paying child support for the past four years? Visiting the boy on a regular basis? Been supportive of Joey in any way since his birth?" Her gaze narrowed. "Has he ever seen his son before today?"

There was a long silence. Aaron could tell Officer Thomas was trying to figure out how to approach the situation. He felt sorry for anyone who was in an adversarial relationship with Maggie. She was one tough cookie.

He should know. She walked away from him with the same disdain emanating from her eyes now.

"I wanna see my kid," Oliver said in a whiny voice. "I got rights."

Maggie didn't say a word, waiting for Officer Thomas to answer.

"No, he has not been doing any of those things," Officer Thomas admitted. "But now that Joey's mother is dead..."

From where he stood several paces behind the officer,

he could see the horror and dread flash across Maggie's features. This was her worst fear.

And he wasn't sure there would be anything she could do to prevent Oliver Chism from taking custody of his son.

"Joey has undergone surgery, and I will not allow him to be upset by being confronted by a stranger." Maggie's gaze pleaded with Officer Thomas to support her in this. "If Mr. Chism is ultimately granted custody of Joey, then obviously we would try to make this as smooth a transition as possible."

"You can't keep me from my kid," Oliver protested.

Maggie ignored him. "Furthermore, I would expect the court to complete a DNA test along with a drug and alcohol assessment of Mr. Chism to make sure he's actually Joey's father and fit to take care of a young child."

The back of Oliver's neck flushed red with anger, or embarrassment. Aaron quickly moved forward to help defuse the situation.

"I agree that Child Protective Services will need to vet Mr. Chism prior to his taking custody of the child," Officer Thomas said. "However, I wasn't sure if Joey needed someone to give consent to medical care. I didn't want there to be a delay in the child getting the care he needs."

Maggie looked as if she might answer, but he stepped in. "Hello, I'm Dr. Aaron Monroe. Unfortunately, Joey's condition took a turn for the worse yesterday," he explained. "The trauma surgeon feared for Joey's life and decided to take him to the operating room after deeming the procedure emergent. He drained the internal bleeding the boy suffered as a result of the bus crash, and he left a drain in place in case more blood accumulated in the area. Joey is also getting IV antibiotics to ward off an infection."

"And that's why I'm not willing to have Joey disturbed

at this time," Maggie added. "He's in pain, and we don't know for sure if he'll need to have another procedure. This is not the time for him to meet his—*father*." The subtle distasteful emphasis on the last word was impossible to ignore. Although Aaron wasn't convinced Oliver Chism was smart enough to pick up on it.

"That is helpful information to know," Officer Thomas said with a nod. "We appreciate the update on Joey's condition. I'm glad to know Joey has been well cared for. And since parental consent is no longer needed, I'll escort Mr. Chism home."

Aaron wondered where the guy lived and made a mental note to call Alec to have him dig into Oliver Chism's background. The guy appeared sketchy, but that didn't mean he had a criminal past.

He had to assume the police wouldn't have brought Oliver Chism to the hospital if he was a felon.

Then again, he wasn't necessarily up to speed on the rules and regulations of family law. Plenty of criminals had kids. The courts didn't intervene unless there was a proven case of neglect or abuse.

The thought of Joey suffering made him angry.

"I'm not leaving till I've seen my kid," Oliver protested. He tried to shake off Officer Thomas's hand.

It didn't work.

"Oh yes, you are," Officer Thomas said. "I'm sure you want to do whatever is in the best interest of your child. Don't you?"

That statement gave the skinny guy pause. As if he was realizing for the first time that his ability to win custody of his son depended on his actions. It was not a guarantee.

"Yeah, sure," Oliver mumbled, hunching his shoulders. "Whatever."

Aaron stepped to the side, giving Officer Thomas and Oliver Chism room to leave. He caught the apologetic expression on the officer's face and knew the guy would be an ally for Joey.

Yet he also knew that the legal system didn't always act in the best interests of the public. If Oliver really was Joey's biological father, the judge might be inclined to place Joey in his custody. Keeping families together was always a top priority.

A soft cry from inside Joey's room had Maggie spinning in the doorway and disappearing inside. He followed, watching as she drew the child into her arms, whispering reassurances.

As before, Joey clung to Maggie like a lifeline. It made sense that the child had gotten so attached to her; she'd barely left his side since the bus crash. When Joey settled back down, she lifted her head to look at him.

"I know," he whispered, easily reading her thoughts. "I'll talk to Alec, see what he can dig up on Chism."

"I'm sure Officer Thomas did that too," she said in a low voice.

"Probably. But Alec is a detective, he may be able to find out more about this guy." He needed to do something to ease the strain on her features. "Let's hope for the best, okay? Maybe he's not as bad as we're assuming he is."

"Maybe." She scowled. "Although I have to believe his mother kept him away from the guy for a reason."

He nodded and pulled out his phone. It was early, but Alec was likely up. He had a seven-year-old daughter named Shannon, and his wife, Jillian, was pregnant again, after suffering a miscarriage. Jillian was fourteen weeks along now, and everyone was praying she would carry this baby to term.

"Hey, Aaron, what's up?" His brother's voice sounded cheerful.

"I need a favor." He turned from the doorway so he wouldn't disturb Joey's sleep. "Remember the work you did last Christmas in finding Joy's mother?"

"Yeah, of course," Alec said. "Do you have an abandoned baby at the hospital again?"

"A little boy has lost his mother in a bus crash," he said. "Joey Johnson is about four years old, and we just got a glimpse of his biological father, Oliver Chism. We're not impressed."

"We?" Alec asked. "Are you working with one of the social workers on the unit?"

"Maggie is in town; we both responded to the bus crash," he said. "She's been with Joey since it happened. He had emergency surgery yesterday and is currently an inpatient here at Children's Memorial."

"Okay." Alec drew the word out. "I'm surprised to hear Maggie is in town, but I'm happy to look into this Oliver Chism character."

"Thanks, Alec. Do you know an Officer Thomas? He was the one who found Oliver Chism listed on Joey's birth certificate."

"Doesn't ring a bell," Alec said. "But I can reach out to him."

He figured it couldn't hurt. "That would be great. Thanks so much. We're really worried about this little boy. He's still struggling with his mother's death."

"I can imagine," Alec murmured. "I'll do my best. I don't suppose you have a middle initial or date of birth for this guy?"

"No. His age is hard to gauge, but I'm assuming

midtwenties? He looks older, and I wouldn't rule out drug or alcohol abuse."

"Got it. I'll see what I can come up with." Alec paused for a moment, then added, "Is Maggie sticking around for a while?"

He turned to look at his ex-wife, snuggled on the hospital bed with Joey as they watched an animated movie. He knew what Alec was really asking. "We're not getting back together or anything, we just want to make sure Joey gets the care he needs."

"Okay." Thankfully, his brother didn't push the issue. "I'll be in touch."

"Thanks." He was about to shove the phone in his pocket when it vibrated with a text message from Jamal.

Grace is being discharged from PACU.

That was his cue to get back to work. For now, he'd done everything he could to help Maggie and Joey.

He could only pray his brother came through for them.

MAGGIE HAD FELT ODDLY bereft when Aaron gave her a nod and walked away. No doubt he needed to follow up on his tiny patient.

As much as she appreciated his calling his brother Alec, she doubted there was much that could be done. Oliver Chism would be considered a suitable custodian for Joey.

Or he wouldn't.

She had been granted a bit of a reprieve but suspected it wouldn't be long until she was forced to introduce the child to his father.

The breakfast she'd shared with Aaron churned in her stomach. But she did her best to stay positive. Joey seemed to be feeling a little better, but when he began to whine, she called the nurse for more pain medication.

The good news was that the little boy was lasting a bit longer between doses. She knew that after the first twenty-four hours, Kyle would likely cut back on the prescribed dose.

And Joey would need to start moving around more too.

"I have'ta go to the bathroom," Joey said.

"Okay, let's go." She helped him into a sitting position, then stood and picked him up from the bed and set him on his feet. During the night, she'd carried him to the bathroom, but now she said, "You know where it is."

He nodded and walked under his own power while she brought the IV pole along. If all went well, the catheter would be removed later that day after his last antibiotic infusion.

Maybe she should feel guilty over the way she'd played up Joey's illness with Officer Thomas, but she didn't. In less than twenty-four hours, the child had lost his mother and had undergone abdominal surgery. Two major life events that were more than enough for the little boy to deal with for now.

Adding a father he'd never met would not help his healing. If anything, she felt certain the little boy would suffer a setback at the thought of being placed with a stranger.

"Hurts," he said, pressing a hand to his side.

"I know." She glanced at her watch, expecting the nurse to arrive with more pain medication any minute. "When you're finished here, I'll check with the nurse."

After going to the bathroom, he frowned, shooting her a resigned look when she made him wash his hands. By the time she had him up in the bed, his nurse had arrived.

The rest of the morning passed slowly. At least for her.

She'd been given a small paper box called a parent pack from the nursing staff. Inside, she'd found basic toiletries, which had enabled her to wash up and brush her teeth without having to return to the hotel. The nursing staff had treated her with a sweet respect, even though they must have known she wasn't Joey's guardian.

Things could have been worse. Yet as much as she intended to stick to Joey like glue, lying stretched out on the hospital bed with the little boy and watching animated movies gave her far too much time to think.

About Aaron. Their failed marriage. And their all-too-civilized divorce.

Odd really, how easily Aaron had given in to her request to separate. At the time, she figured he'd fully intended to move on with some other woman who could give him the six Monroe kids he'd wanted, but he hadn't.

Maybe he was more married to his career than she'd realized. After all, the way he was constantly texting with the residents during their time off work had been incredibly annoying.

It didn't matter, so why was she ruminating over those last few fateful weeks in her mind?

Because seeing Aaron again after two years had reminded her of the good times they'd shared, more so than the bad times.

She still couldn't quite figure out why Aaron was still single. Or so she assumed since he hadn't mentioned he was seeing anyone.

Just like she wasn't seeing anyone either.

Would Aaron come and find her when he heard from his brother Alec? She knew without hesitation he would. And thinking of Alec made her wonder how the rest of his family was doing. Tragic to hear how Andrea had lost her husband, but knowing the others were all married was interesting. She had no doubt they were all starting families of their own.

A family she and Aaron could never have.

Enough. There was no point in thinking about what might have been. Better to stay focused on why God had put her outside the Pfister Hotel as the truck had plowed into the bus.

If not for that, she wouldn't be sitting here with Joey now. Contemplating how she could finagle a way to become his temporary, then permanent guardian.

Rather than his father. The thought made her wince. Did she really think she was that much better than Oliver Chism?

Yeah, she did. But that wasn't fair. It was entirely possible the guy hadn't known about Joey. His mother may have decided to keep him a secret.

But then why list him on the birth certificate?

Thinking about Oliver Chism made her head hurt.

"Dr. Dall?" A pretty woman poked her head into the room. "I'm Eloise from social services. I understand you requested a consult?"

"Yes." She glanced down to see Joey was still awake, albeit focused on the television screen. "I need to talk to Eloise for a few minutes, okay?"

"'Kay," Joey said with a yawn. Clearly the pain meds were keeping him mellow.

She slipped from the bed and stretched before moving toward the door. She was not accustomed to sitting around all day, and her muscles were starting to scream in protest. She stepped out into the hall so Joey wouldn't overhear.

"I understand you're interested in becoming a foster parent for Joseph Johnson," Eloise said.

"Yes, I am." She had asked for this meeting yesterday, before she'd known about Oliver Chism being Joey's biological father. Still, she wasn't about to simply hand the child over without a fight. Or at least knowing Oliver would treat the boy well. "I was hoping you could help me navigate the process."

"I can, but you know it takes time. And you don't live in Wisconsin anymore, is that correct?" Eloise glanced at the tablet in her hand. "I don't know that any judge will approve a foster mother from out of state."

"I grew up in this area and can move back easily enough," she said. "That's not important. Finding a proper guardian for Joey is all that matters."

"Yes, of course. That's what we want too," Eloise hastened to reassure her.

Maggie sighed and knew she couldn't keep crucial information from this woman. It wasn't as if she wouldn't find out sooner or later anyway. "You should know that police officer Thomas came by earlier with a man by the name of Oliver Chism. It's possible he's Joey's father."

"Oh, I see." Eloise's glance was sympathetic. "That changes things."

"Only if a DNA test proves he's Joey's father and if he is deemed fit to care for a young child," Maggie said. "Getting those results back will likely take time, which is why I would still like to begin the process of being a temporary foster parent for Joey."

"Hmm." Eloise didn't look convinced.

"I have been at his side, holding and caring for him since the accident." She tried not to sound as desperate as she felt. "He trusts me and has been leaning on me for support. Don't make him start over with someone new. Not yet. Not until we know for sure Mr. Chism is his actual father and capable of caring for him."

Eloise sighed and nodded. "There's no reason you can't start the process by filling out the paperwork online." She handed Maggie the tablet. "You can use this. I have the site bookmarked for you. However, you have to understand that today is Saturday. No one will even look at this application until Monday. And even then..." She shrugged. "You know how government stuff works. Nothing moves at warp speed. You'll have to make some phone calls if you want this to be treated as a priority."

"I understand. Thank you." She clutched the tablet to her chest. "I'll get this back to you as soon as possible."

"I'm here until three o'clock this afternoon." Eloise offered a gentle smile. "I hope this works out for you."

"Me too." And wasn't that the understatement of the year? She turned to head back into Joey's room. Then she settled on the bed next to the little boy to begin filling out the government form. She shouldn't have been surprised that the entire process took well over an hour to complete.

And even then, she went back through the form to make sure she hadn't missed anything.

She pressed submit, then let out a soundless sigh. The first step had been completed.

All she could do now was wait.

And pray.

CHAPTER SEVEN

After checking in on Grace, who was doing very well post-op from her procedure and settled in the pediatric ICU, Aaron decided he couldn't put off speaking with Dale Fullerton any longer. As much as he detested the need to address his colleague, patient care had to be a priority.

Maggie had once accused him of avoiding conflict, and she was probably right about that. He preferred to get along with people, ignoring the drama.

But he couldn't ignore this. Not when there might be a time when Aaron wasn't in the city to take care of an emergency if Dale decided he didn't feel like answering his pager or his phone.

He headed to his office and took the time to make himself another cup of coffee with the single-cup machine. Then he settled into the leather chair behind his desk and reached for the landline phone. He paged Fullerton through the normal process, as if he was one of the residents up on the floor. He'd thought Fullerton might recognize his office number and answer anyway, but he didn't. Gritting his teeth, he called the surgeon directly, knowing his name and number would flash on Fullerton's cell phone screen.

Fullerton didn't answer, letting the call go through to voicemail. Maybe he'd done that on purpose because of his failure to respond to the earlier page. After all, Fullerton had to make it look as if his phone was off or not working properly.

Sure enough, less than ten minutes later, Aaron's cell phone rang. Seeing Fullerton's name, he didn't bother with niceties. "Where have you been?" he demanded. He hadn't intended to start off this way, but his anger and frustration boiled over. "I had to take a six-month-old baby to the OR because you didn't answer your pages."

"I—I'm sorry. My phone was on silent." Fullerton sounded concerned. "I had no idea that a baby was in trouble."

"And what's wrong with your pager? Dead battery?" He didn't hide the snark in his tone. "Give me a break. This is not the first time you haven't responded to calls on a weekend, and I'm fed up with others having to cover your lapse. This time, I'm taking formal disciplinary action against you."

"What? You can't do that! Just because I missed a few pages!" Now Fullerton sounded angry.

"Watch me. I took a little girl to surgery because you didn't answer your phone or your pager." He enunciated each word carefully as if explaining this to a dimwit. "That's dereliction of duty. You should have been here doing your job. But you weren't. Be in my office first thing Monday morning. I'll arrange for a meeting with the chief of staff."

"Now wait a minute!" There was a note of panic in

Fullerton's tone. "There's no need to go off the deep end just because I accidentally put my phone on silent—"

"It's too late for excuses," he interrupted. Maybe he was tired and stressed over the situation with Maggie and Joey, not to mention having to come in early, but he was not budging on this. "You're relieved of duty until further notice. I'll cover your call for the rest of the weekend since I've been here since three in the morning anyway."

There was a long moment of silence as if the reality of the situation was finally sinking into Dale Fullerton's tiny brain. Dale's voice was subdued when he spoke again. "I'll be happy to cover your next weekend on call in exchange for you working this weekend."

Yeah, nice try, he thought. "Monday morning. My office at seven a.m. Don't be late." Aaron quickly ended the call. After setting his cell phone aside, he scrubbed his hands over his face. Why had he taken a leadership role?

Oh yeah, because it seemed like a good idea at the time.

With a sigh, he sipped his coffee. Then he sent a flurry of emails. First, he made sure to remove Fullerton from the call schedule, then he made sure the chief of staff, Dr. Rob Kent, would be able to attend the Monday morning meeting. Finally, he went back through his notes to document the four times in six months that Fullerton had not answered his calls.

When those administrative tasks were finished, he downed the last of his coffee and rose to his feet. He'd make rounds on the cardiac surgery patients, then head home.

To his empty house.

Turning away from his troubled thoughts, he ran a report of all cardiac surgery patients within the hospital. Then he began making rounds, pleased to note that most of their tiny patients were doing fine. One patient happened to be on Joey's unit, and he had to force himself to walk past the little boy's room without poking his head in to see Maggie.

He needed to stop letting her mess with his head. She wasn't in town to see him. She'd attended a conference, responded to a bus crash, and jumped in to help support a scared and injured little boy.

If not for the crash, Maggie would be back in Boston right now doing whatever she did on her weekends off.

Dating? He hid a wince as he logged into the next patient chart. Why wouldn't she be dating? She was beautiful, smart, and single.

The next few hours dragged by with excruciating slowness. Knowing Maggie was there made it difficult to get back into his usual routine.

At home, he flipped through TV stations to find the Big Ten college football game. But after several minutes, he realized he had no idea who was playing or what the score was.

When his phone rang, he startled badly. Expecting the call to be from the hospital, he was surprised to see Alec's number on the screen. "Hey, Alec. Don't tell me you found something on Oliver Chism already?"

"Bro, it's been five hours since you called," Alec drawled. "So yeah, I spent time digging into your guy. And you're right about his history of drug abuse. I found a court-ordered rehab from last year after he crashed his car into a tree."

He took a moment to digest that information. "I guess he could be clean since that happened."

"Doubtful," Alec drawled. "He was arrested six months

ago with possession. He wasn't carrying a lot of weight, just a couple ounces of crack cocaine, but he spent another month in jail before he was released on parole."

"What impact does his being on parole have on his ability to be granted custody of his son?" To Aaron's mind, it should be a no-brainer for the judge to rule against giving Chism custody of Joey. Why take the risk of Chism falling back into his old ways? And how did a drug addict support himself anyway?

"Depends on the judge," Alec said. "If custody is granted, someone from Child Protective Services would be expected to make frequent home visits to make sure Chism was treating his son well."

"Home visits." He shook his head in disgust. "Anyone can pull it together long enough to pass a home visit."

"Not if he's using again," Alec said. "And my impression is that the home visits are not scheduled ahead of time."

"Yeah, okay." He didn't like it, but getting mad at Alec wouldn't help. "Would the judge mandate drug testing too?"

"Yes, that's part of being out on parole." Alec was silent for a moment. "I wish I could reassure you that Chism won't get custody, but there are too many variables at play to know how things will shake out. I'm sorry."

"Yeah, I know." It was Joey who would suffer the most if things didn't work out with his father. "I appreciate you digging into the guy for me. I feel bad taking you away from your family on a Saturday."

"No problem, I took time off for Shannon's soccer game." Alec chuckled softly. "Gotta say, she plays with heart, even if there isn't a whole lot of skill."

"She's young, give her time," Aaron said. He'd liked

being closer to his parents, but seeing the happy families of his siblings was bittersweet. Yet he had nothing to complain about, seeing as Andrea had lost her husband.

He and Andrea had bonded over their respective losses at the last family dinner. Andrea had her two kids, Bethany and Ben, to help keep her busy.

He didn't have anything but his work to distract him from his loss.

"I'm not complaining," Alec said. "If Shannon is happy, that's all that matters."

"Yeah, I hear you." He thought briefly about the kids he'd never have. "Hey, do you mind throwing a quick summary together on what you've discovered about Oliver Chism? I think that might come in handy down the road."

"Sure thing. I'll send it along later today," Alec agreed. There was a brief pause, then Alec added, "Be careful, Aaron. You're allowing yourself to get personally involved with this kid. Much the way Adam did last Christmas with baby Joy."

"I know. It must be something in the Monroe DNA, though, because I can't turn my back on this little boy's situation. Thanks again, Alec. Spend the rest of your day off with your family."

"I will. Later." Alec ended the call without saying anything more.

But as Aaron stared at his phone, he realized probably would not have been as emotionally invested in Joey's care if not for Maggie's involvement.

Maybe he wasn't as good of a person as Adam. And that knowledge sat like a rock in his gut, making him wonder if he was the real reason Maggie had left.

Not her inability to bear a child.

THE HOURS MAGGIE spent at Joey's bedside passed with an odd routine. The pain meds made him fall asleep, but in between doses, she'd encouraged him to get out of bed and move around. It was heartbreaking how Joey tried to please her, and tears rolled down her cheeks when she thought about handing him over to his father.

At two o'clock in the afternoon, Kyle Flores came into the room to check on Joey's abdominal drain. "How are you feeling?" he asked the little boy.

"Sometimes my tummy hurts," Joey said. "'Specially when I move. But I got to watch *Aladdin*! It was so good."

Kyle smiled as he took his stethoscope from his pocket and used it to listen to Joey's heart and lungs. "I'm glad you're moving around; it's important you walk in the halls with your—er, Maggie."

Joey nodded, but his gaze had been drawn back to the television screen. Another animated movie was playing now, one she didn't recognize.

"His lungs sound good," Kyle said. "You've been doing a great job of keeping him quiet and active at the same time."

"I honestly had no idea how difficult a task that would be," she said with a wry smile. "If not for the pain holding him back, I think he'd be bouncing off the walls."

"Spoken like a true parent," he said. "I need to double-check how much drainage he's had since surgery."

"The same as I told you earlier, roughly ten milliliters." She couldn't blame him for logging into the computer to see the information for himself. "Nothing from the drain since zero six hundred."

"I keep forgetting you're a physician," he said, turning to smile at her. "Okay, I think we can safely remove the drain." He logged out of the computer, then reached for a pair of gloves from the box mounted on the wall. "I'll need you to hold Joey still for a minute while I do that."

"Of course." She wasn't going anywhere.

Kyle didn't ask for help from the nurse or delegate the task to a resident. He opened a clean dressing and set it off to the side, then glanced down at Joey. She lifted Joey's hospital gown and began working the tape from his skin.

Thankfully, Joey was so enamored of the show he didn't pay much attention. When she had the tape off, she tightened her grip on the little boy.

With a smooth, swift movement, Kyle pulled the drain and covered the opening with a fresh dressing. She held the white gauze in place as he disposed of the drain, then stripped off his gloves.

"He didn't even notice," she murmured.

"It's a good thing," Kyle agreed. He taped the dressing down, then stepped back. "He has one more dose of antibiotic to get, then we can get rid of the IV too."

"I guess that means he'll be ready for discharge soon." She frowned. "How does that work on a weekend when there's no legal guardian?"

"I was planning to keep him inpatient until Monday," Kyle said. "It won't hurt to give him an extra day here, especially being a weekend. I need to see how he tolerates food too. I've written orders for him to start with clear liquids tonight, and if he does well with Jell-O and popsicles, we can move into full liquids by morning. I've also written orders to have the social worker talk to Child Protective Services first thing Monday morning to discuss our next steps with Joey's discharge."

A wave of panic hit hard. There was no way she'd be approved to be Joey's foster parent by Monday afternoon.

Logically, she'd known it wasn't likely she'd be able to stay with Joey after his discharge, but hearing it now felt like she'd been hit by a brick.

Since Kyle was looking at her expectantly, she nodded. "I understand."

"Maggie." He rested a hand on her shoulder. "You've developed a bond with Joey. He's doing really well, and I'm happy to let the representative from Child Protective Services know that if needed."

"Thanks. It's just...I feel bad for him." She managed a smile. "He's been through a lot, and the thought of handing him over to a stranger..."

"I know." Kyle looked as if he wanted to say something more, but then he turned back to the computer. He logged on, probably to write a note about removing the drain and updating his orders. When he finished, he turned back to face her. "You should know that most of the foster parents I've run across are kind and caring people. No matter how this turns out, I'm sure Joey will do fine."

Easy for him to say, he hadn't met Joey's father. But he had a point about the foster care system. Every profession in the world had a few bad apples in the bunch, but focusing on the negative was silly. She could stick around in Milwaukee to make sure Joey was assigned someone decent.

The bigger concern was Oliver Chism. She couldn't bear the thought of Oliver getting custody of Joey long term. There had to be a way to prevent that, but how, she wasn't sure. Especially if the guy had managed to clean up his act.

"Thanks, Kyle. You've been great through this."

"You're welcome. I'll see you again in the morning," he promised, before heading out of the room.

She smoothed Joey's hair back from his forehead, her thoughts whirling. She'd need to request a personal leave of absence from work so she could stay in town longer. At least she had the hotel room, but depending on where Joey was placed on Monday, she may need something different.

Either a rental house where she could have a bedroom for the little boy to use or another hotel closer to wherever his foster parents lived.

Was she crazy to be doing this? Kyle was a decent guy, and he wasn't getting all wrapped up in Joey's future the way she was.

Yes, she'd taken him from his dying mother's arms and held him close. Yes, he'd bonded with her—out of necessity as he was injured too. Yes, she'd stayed the night with him to make sure he didn't have a relapse.

But right now he was content watching cartoons. And one thing she'd learned during her years of being a pediatric anesthesiologist was that kids were incredibly resilient. Joey was only four years old; he may not even remember his time with her once he was placed in a loving home with parents who adored him.

She was the one making a bigger deal out of his future. As if becoming Joey's foster mother was the only acceptable option.

How many other kids in this hospital didn't have parents? Probably more than she wanted to know. If circumstances were such that she couldn't be there for Joey, there was nothing to stop her from returning to Boston and going through the process there to become a foster parent. The hoops she'd need to jump through couldn't be that much different.

Yet somehow Joey had taken hold of her heart.

"Hey, do you want to try a popsicle?" she asked.

Joey glanced at her and nodded. "I like purple the best."

"I'll see what I can do." She slid from the bed and

walked out into the hallway. There was no sign of Joey's nurse, so she found the kitchenette and peeked into the freezer. Just as she'd suspected, there were plenty of popsicles inside. Although finding a grape one wasn't as easy. It must have been a popular flavor because she had to dig way down into the plastic bag to find one.

On her way back to Joey's room, a familiar man stood in the hallway. Her stomach clenched as she hurried forward. "Mr. Chism? What are you doing here?"

"I deserve to see my son." He sneered, bolder now that Officer Thomas wasn't standing beside him.

"I'm sorry, but that's not possible." She kept her voice even with an effort, hoping she wouldn't have to get into a physical altercation with the guy. A quick glance confirmed they were alone in this section of the hallway.

As if sensing her fear, Chism took a threatening step toward her. "Who's gonna stop me? You?"

"If I have to," she said calmly. "But I don't think you want me to call Officer Thomas to let him know that you are not acting in your son's best interest. Something I'm sure the judge in family court would not like to hear."

His narrow gaze pierced hers for a long moment as he seemed to consider what she'd said. She hoped he'd turn and walk away, yet the fact that he'd even shown up in the first place was concerning.

She could only imagine he'd thought he could bully her into allowing him to visit, or he'd assumed she wouldn't still be there.

Wrong on both counts. She edged closer, putting herself between Oliver and Joey's door.

Where were the nurses? Or better yet, a security guard? Surely, Children's Memorial had them the same way they did in Boston.

"I talked to a lawyer," Chism said.

Already? She wondered what kind of lawyer he could get calling on a Saturday. "I'm sure you have. But you shouldn't be here now. Joey needs his rest."

"You can't keep me from getting my kid," Chism sneered. "My lawyer says we're getting big bucks from the bus accident."

He'd spoken to a personal injury lawyer? She wasn't sure if she should laugh or cry. The lawyer handling the bus crash would not be the same one to represent Oliver Chism in family court.

But it made sense now why he'd risked coming back to the hospital. Oliver was seeing Joey as his payday.

"Maggie? Is there a problem?"

She turned to see Aaron striding toward them, concern etched on his features. She smiled in relief and quickly nodded. "Mr. Chism seems to think he can see Joey whenever he wants. I'll need you to reach out to Officer Thomas. I know you have his phone number."

"Absolutely," Aaron agreed. "I'll call him right now."

"I'm going. I'm going." Apparently, Oliver wasn't in the mood to speak with Officer Thomas again. The skinny, twitchy man finally took a step back. He flashed an eerie smile. "But I'll be back. My lawyer says I have rights."

She nodded, waiting for him to turn and leave. When Chism was gone, Aaron asked, "How in the world did he get a lawyer so fast?"

"It's not what you think. He has a personal injury lawyer. He probably called one of those numbers on the billboards along the freeway." She sighed and gestured to Joey's room. "I need to give him this popsicle before it melts. Then I'll fill you in."

"Of course." He held the door for her. As she gave Joey

his popsicle, which thankfully wasn't as melted as she had feared, she was glad Aaron had arrived when he did.

Yet it was odd that Aaron was proving to be more supportive of her now that they were divorced than when they were married.

CHAPTER EIGHT

Lingering in Joey's room wasn't smart, especially watching Maggie and Joey interact as if they were mother and son when that wasn't the likely outcome here. Yet Aaron was loath to leave.

"Kyle came by and removed Joey's drain." Maggie offered a sad smile. "Joey's recovery is going well. And while that's good news, it looks like Joey will be ready for discharge on Monday."

He nodded thoughtfully. "That's not a lot of time to get a foster parent arranged."

"Tell me about it." She grimaced. "I filled out the application, but I'm sure there's no way I'll get approved that quickly."

He wasn't surprised she'd filled out the application, although he didn't understand why she even tried. "You don't live here, Maggie. I can't imagine a judge is going to approve you taking him to Boston."

"I know, I thought I could get a rental property for a few months while I look for a job here in the Milwaukee area."

Wait, she was planning to move back here? He stared at

her for a long moment. "I don't know what to say. That's a huge move when you don't know for sure how this will turn out." *This* being Joey's biological father.

If Oliver Chism was, in fact, Joey's biological father. He'd want to see the DNA results for himself before letting that guy near the boy.

Then again, if Chism was able to get a lawyer, he and Maggie may have little say in the matter. Joey's mother did list the guy as the father on the birth certificate. Seems unlikely she would have done that if it wasn't true.

"I know it's a big move, but I need to try." Maggie glanced at Joey who licked his popsicle while watching television. The boy didn't seem to be paying much attention to the adults in the room. "I can't just walk away."

"You walked away from us," he said, before he could check himself.

She flushed and crossed her arms over her chest. "You let me. And besides, you know I can't give you the family you wanted."

He was about to point out that all he'd wanted was her and to maybe adopt when his phone rang. Seeing Jamal's number on the screen, he groaned. "Sorry, I have to take this."

"I know." Maggie turned her attention to Joey while he walked out of the room to take the call.

"What's going on with Grace?" he asked.

"She's got some bleeding, and I thought you'd want to come and see for yourself." Jamal sounded more concerned than panicked, but he trusted the resident's judgment.

"I'll be right over." He lowered his phone, wishing he could stay and finish this conversation with Maggie. "My post-op patient is bleeding. I'm sorry. I need to go see her."

"Don't apologize." Maggie said the words casually, but her expression was tense. "I know patient care comes first."

Did she? He hesitated, then forced himself to turn away. Their relationship was over, and covering old ground wouldn't change anything.

No matter how much he wanted it to.

As he headed to the pediatric ICU, he quickly called Alec. "Hey, Oliver Chism showed up here at Children's Memorial to see his son despite being told not to."

"You want me to follow him around?" Alec asked. "Maybe I can catch him in the act of committing a crime."

That sounded drastic, and while it was tempting, he knew it wasn't fair. It was Saturday, and Alec had a family of his own. "No, I guess I was looking for advice. Not sure what we can do to keep him out of the hospital while Joey recovers from his surgery."

"I can talk to a friend of mine who happens to work in the police district where Chism lives," Alec offered. "Cops often know the troublemakers who ride the line in their district. Maybe he has some ideas."

"Thanks. Whatever you can do that doesn't take you away from Shannon and Jillian is great."

"You got it," Alec said. "Later."

"Later." He pocketed his phone as he entered the intensive care unit. Jamal was standing at Grace's bedside, his expression somber. The six-month-old baby girl was connected to monitors, but he looked at her first, looking at her cute face and the way her chest rose and fell with each breath before lifting his gaze to the blood pressure and heart rate readings across the screen.

"She's tachy, and her BP is low," Jamal said, stating the obvious. "I've been watching her closely but wanted to make sure you were in the loop."

"I appreciate that." From his perspective, the baby's condition was stable, but if the bleeding didn't slow down soon, she'd fall into the critical category. "I'll stay here for a while if you have other patients to see."

Jamal hesitated, then nodded. "Thanks. You know how weekends are. My pager has been going off a lot. I've done most of the troubleshooting over the phone, but there are a couple of patients I should see in person. Although none as sick as Grace."

"Go ahead, I'll watch Grace." He frowned. "If she needs to go back to the OR, I'll let you know."

Jamal looked relieved until his pager went off again. With a sigh, the resident left the PICU, no doubt needing to check on yet another crisis.

He settled in beside Grace, debating the pros and cons of giving the baby a blood transfusion. Normally, he avoided going down that path. In his experience, kids typically recovered fairly well without them. And transfusions were not without risk; he'd seen his share of transfusion reactions. He'd had one young patient who'd nearly died after experiencing a transfusion reaction. It was a case where he'd decided at the last minute to stay in the room to watch over the patient himself. If he hadn't? He was convinced the little boy wouldn't have survived.

Hence why he tended to wait before ordering what some surgeons considered a routine treatment. Yet he didn't like how pale Grace was. Or the way her vitals teetered on the verge of crashing.

He settled in to wait and watch. He'd give her another thirty minutes before making his decision. Unless her condition changed to the point he had no choice.

At times like this, he wondered why he'd become a pediatric cardiac surgeon.

This level of responsibility—holding the life of a six-month-old baby in your hands—was not for the faint-hearted.

MAGGIE DIDN'T SEE Aaron again for the rest of Saturday night, which ironically bothered her. Not that she'd wanted to rehash the circumstances of their divorce, but the fact that he'd accused her of walking away stung.

She hadn't seen it that way. She'd told him to move on and to have the family he deserved. He hadn't, and now she wanted to know why.

Did he still have feelings for her?

The way she still loved him?

Sleep didn't come easy. By Sunday morning, she would have given a lot for a giant cup of coffee. Joey was doing better, but he still woke up crying in pain when the medication wore off. She was exhausted yet relieved to see Joey was eager to try some pudding. He'd handled the Jell-O and popsicles well last night, which enabled him to move on to a full liquid diet. Hopefully by dinner time, he could try solid foods.

She'd tried to get him to eat the oatmeal, but he was not having it. Hard to argue, as oatmeal was no match for chocolate pudding.

When he was finished with his breakfast, she stood and stretched her sore muscles before setting the empty tray aside so he could color. It was nice to see him doing something other than watching Disney+. With a yawn, she blinked the exhaustion from her eyes. She'd slept on the cot in the room between rounds of holding Joey in her arms to help him drift off to sleep.

She'd always known the hospital setting wasn't the best place to get rest. Frequent interruptions during the night prevented that. Experiencing it firsthand was a whole new level of frustration. She'd finally convinced the nurse to not wake Joey to take vital signs, but to wait until he needed more pain medication. If it wasn't exactly every four hours, too bad. The nurse had reluctantly agreed. That one change had provided her almost three full hours of sleep.

Not great, but better than nothing.

"Where's my mommy?" Joey's innocent question was like a knife slicing through her heart. She'd explained this several times, but he was only four and likely couldn't comprehend the concept of death.

"Your mommy is up in heaven with God and Jesus," she said.

"When is she coming back?" Joey asked, glancing up from his coloring book. "I want her to come see me."

This was the hardest thing she'd ever done, and no matter how she tried to say the words, she couldn't soften the blow. "Your mommy can't come back, Joey. She's in heaven forever."

His lower lip trembled. "I want my mommy."

"I know, sweetie. I know." She sat on the edge of his mattress and cuddled him close. Now that the IV tubing had been removed, he could move more freely. He wrapped his arms around her neck, holding on tight. "Your mommy loved you very much," she whispered.

He didn't say anything in response but buried his face against her chest. This was why she'd submitted the paperwork to become a foster parent. And why she'd uproot her life and her career to relocate here to Milwaukee if that helped her get custody of Joey.

This little boy needed her in a way no one else ever had.

Not even Aaron.

Comparing a child's need for a mother figure wasn't the same as the bond between husband and wife, but Aaron hadn't really needed her. Maybe it was his being the oldest sibling, but he always seemed to be in control, taking charge and rarely showing signs of weakness. The day she'd sat him down to explain her most recent fertility testing results proved she'd never have a child, he'd offered up the idea of adoption while texting his colleagues at the hospital about a patient.

And like today, he'd had to leave before things could be resolved. She'd known then that Aaron hadn't really wanted to adopt. He'd only mentioned it to make her feel better. His focus had been on his career.

His skilled hands had saved countless children's lives. He was probably the best pediatric cardiac surgeon in the country, but she'd wanted more from him. She'd hoped he'd feel the loss of never having a child together as acutely as she had.

But he hadn't. He'd moved onto the next task, his next patient, the next crisis, leaving her to realize their marriage was over. He'd thought walking away had been easy for her.

It hadn't been easy by any stretch of the imagination. But after she'd moved out, he'd agreed to her request for a divorce without an argument.

Whatever. She gave herself a mental shake. Seeing Aaron nonstop over these past two days had drudged up the old anger and resentment. Useless emotions that were not a part of her future.

And not part of Aaron's future either.

When Joey finally fell asleep, she'd taken advantage of the time to grab coffee and a breakfast sandwich from the cafeteria. She'd half expected to run into Aaron, but she hadn't. No doubt he was at home, or maybe up on one of the patient care units seeing patients.

She ate the sandwich in record time, then carried her coffee back to Joey's room. He was still sleeping, zonked from the pain meds, so she curled into the recliner.

She must have dozed herself, despite the caffeine, because she heard a soft voice asking, "Maggie? Are you Maggie Dall?"

"Hmm?" She opened her eyes to find a beautiful woman with long dark hair pulled into a ponytail, big brown eyes, and wearing teddy-bear scrubs hovering in the doorway of Joey's room. Glancing at the child to make sure he was still sleeping, she nodded and rose from the recliner to meet with the woman she assumed was one of the nurses who worked there. "Yes. I'm Maggie Dall."

"I'm Krista Monroe, Adam's wife." She gestured for Maggie to step outside the room. "Adam suggested I stop in and chat with you while I was on break."

"Ah, okay." She was still sleep deprived, so it took her a minute to put the puzzle pieces together. Adam was Aaron's second oldest brother who was also a pediatrician. She had never met Krista and didn't know anything about her. "Do you work here? On this floor?"

"I work on six south," Krista explained. "That unit handles babies up to two years old."

"I see." She was at a loss as to what Krista wanted. It would be one thing if she and Aaron were still married, but they weren't. "That must be challenging. At least older kids can tell you when something hurts."

"Very challenging, but I love it." Krista smiled. "That's one of the reasons I wanted to stop by."

"Oh?" Maggie tried to follow her line of thought. "If

you're worried about Joey Johnson, there's no need. He's doing much better today."

"I understand he lost his mother in the bus crash," Krista said. "And that you're interested in being his foster parent."

For a moment, she was struck by a flash of annoyance. Did the whole hospital know about her? Then she realized Krista was here because Aaron had spoken to Adam. She managed a smile. "Yes, that's true. Unfortunately, I don't think I'll be able to make that happen. For one thing, Joey's biological father wants custody. Besides, I haven't moved back to Milwaukee yet, so I don't know that the family court judge would agree to providing me temporary guardianship."

"His dad, huh?" Krista frowned. "Is he able to care for Joey?"

"That's the million-dollar question," Maggie said with a sigh. "I have my not-so-favorable opinion as he's never been involved in Joey's life, not even in making child-care payments to Joey's mother. Yet I'm aware that judges often lean toward keeping families together." It pained her to speak the truth. "Unless Oliver Chism has done something terrible, I suspect he has a good chance of getting custody of his son."

"I see." Krista pursed her lips. "One good thing about your situation is that it takes time to work through the legal system. I think the court will err on the side of caution when it comes to placing a child who recently had surgery with a man who's never been a part of his life."

She wanted to hug Krista for saying that. "I would like to think so too."

"I have already been approved as a foster parent," Krista

said. "Adam and I can take Joey in while the process plays out."

"You are?" Maggie was shocked to hear it. Then she remembered Aaron saying something about his brother Adam and a safe haven baby. She had told him she planned to apply to be Joey's foster mother, yet it was humbling to know Krista was here offering to help. "I—don't know what to say. That's very nice of you and would be very helpful as far as making sure Joey is placed with good people who will care about him."

"Exactly," Krista agreed. "We would be happy to welcome Joey into our home."

It was the perfect solution, but Maggie couldn't seem to grasp the opportunity with both hands. Maybe it was selfish of her, but she wanted to be Joey's foster mother.

And possibly his permanent mother, if Chism wasn't Joey's biological father.

"My biggest concern for Joey is that he's become rather attached to me." Maggie tried to put her feelings into words. "I realize that is only because I happened to respond to the bus crash," she admitted. "I've stayed with him from the scene of the crash, getting him through surgery, and now his recovery. But he hasn't warmed up to the other nursing staff."

"I understand. I had a very similar experience last Christmas with baby Joy." Krista smiled gently. "I was thrilled that Joy was able to be reunited with her mother, but I can't deny it was hard to let her go. Watching Joy's mother hold her close helped make the transition easier for me."

There was a vast difference from what Krista was describing and her situation. She couldn't even imagine

Oliver Chism taking Joey in his arms and holding the boy while he fell asleep.

"Anyway, I just wanted to let you know that I'll reach out to the department of Child Protective Services first thing on Monday morning," Krista said. "I'll get the ball rolling. And you are, of course, welcome to stay with me and Adam to help care for Joey. We have plenty of room in our new home."

"I—okay." She managed a wan smile. As painful as it was to admit, this was probably the best solution for Joey's future. Far better than leaving the little boy with a stranger. "That's very kind of you."

"We're happy to help." Krista looked over Maggie's shoulder toward the sleeping boy. "I'm sure that poor boy has been through a lot. He deserves all the love and support we can provide."

Maggie nodded because Krista was right. She couldn't let her personal feelings get in the way of whatever was in Joey's best interest. "I don't know much about how kids his age process death, but I have been thinking of asking a child psychologist for advice. I figure there must be one on staff here that I can reach out to."

"That's a great idea," Krista agreed. Her gaze was somber. "What have you told him so far?"

"Just that his mother has died and went to heaven to be with God and Jesus." She grimaced. "He's only four years old, and from what I can tell, he hasn't grasped the concept of his mother never coming back."

"We definitely need input from a child psychologist," Krista said with a sigh. "I honestly don't know how else to tell him about his mother either."

"I was thinking that maybe we could get some pictures of his mother from their apartment, if the police will allow it." Maggie had intended to ask Officer Thomas about that, but his showing up with Joey's father had caused her to forget. "At least the pictures might help him remember her."

"Maybe it's better he doesn't remember her," Krista said. Then she winced. "I don't mean to sound harsh, but it might be easier for him to accept a new mother figure so he can move forward with his young life than to ruminate on his loss."

Maggie nodded. It was nice to have another person to share ideas with about the best way to approach Joey's care. "I'm open to whatever the child psychologist recommends."

"Tell Joey's nurse to put in a consult," Krista advised. Then she glanced at her watch. "Sorry, but I need to get back."

"Of course." Maggie knew hospitals remained busy on the weekends. Sometimes more so than during the week. "Thanks for coming by."

"Why don't you give me your phone number?" Krista pulled out her cell. "That way we can keep in touch."

Maggie gave Krista her number, then took hers, too, bemused at how quickly she'd bonded with her former brother-in-law's wife. "Thanks, Krista."

"See you tomorrow," Krista promised, before hurrying away.

Maggie returned to Joey's room as the little boy was waking up from his nap. As she helped him walk to the bathroom, she couldn't help feeling as if a huge weight had been taken off her shoulders.

Krista and Adam were good people. And if she couldn't be Joey's foster mother, Krista was the next best thing.

Yet somehow it made her sad to know she probably wouldn't have to move back to Milwaukee after all.

Sad to know that once she returned to Boston, she wouldn't see Aaron again.

CHAPTER NINE

Aaron had ended up giving Grace a transfusion, which thankfully she tolerated well. Since she was doing better, he'd finally headed home, even though he'd had to forcibly turn around and stop himself from going up to the seventh floor to see Maggie.

He'd made rounds again on Sunday but then joined his family at church. Again, he'd managed to get in and out of Children's Memorial without stopping in to see Maggie.

His parents had brunch at their house. Andrea seemed to be doing better, as were her two kids, Bethany and Ben. Shannon was there, too, close in age to Bethany. He spent time with his nieces and nephew, keenly aware of what he was missing out on.

The family he'd always thought he'd have with Maggie.

"Hey, do you have a minute?" Alec asked in a low tone.

"Sure." He disentangled himself from the kids and followed Alec outside where they could talk in private. Aaron hadn't wanted his parents to learn Maggie was in town, fearing they'd anticipate a reconciliation.

"So I heard from Jack earlier this morning about that address you gave me for that guy, Oliver Chism."

"Jack is your cop friend, right?"

"Yeah, Jack Waldon. Anyway, he is very familiar with that address. The building houses low-income rental units, and while there are plenty of good people who live there, Jack said they've responded to multiple calls related to drug deals and prostitution."

Somehow, Aaron wasn't surprised by that. "But no arrests where Oliver Chism was involved?"

"No. But I told him to keep an eye out on the guy." Alec shrugged. "Maybe Chism will screw up."

"Yeah, maybe." He wasn't about to bank on it, though. Especially not when Chism is seeing dollar signs related to Joey's accident. He was cynical enough to think that the potential settlement along with governmental support were the main drivers behind Chism's actions regarding his son. "Thanks, Alec. I appreciate your buddy keeping an eye out for this guy."

"I can always follow him if needed," Alec said with a grin. "It might be fun. I enjoy my new role as being a detective, but I wouldn't mind getting back out on the street."

"No need," he said. "I'm sure you have plenty of other stuff to do."

"If you change your mind, let me know." Alec pinned him with a serious gaze. "How are you really? I'm surprised Maggie is here in town."

Aaron grimaced. "Yeah, her showing up was a shock. Seeing her is reopening old wounds." Thankfully, his pager went off. "I better take this."

"Yeah, sure." Alec turned to head back inside.

For the next couple of hours, Aaron fielded several calls.

Nothing that required him to head back to the hospital, which was probably a good thing.

After brunch, he went home to pull his notes together on Dale Fullerton in preparation for the Monday morning meeting. By the time he'd finished, he felt confident he had more than enough proof of Fullerton's dereliction of duty.

The question remained, though, whether Chief of Staff Rob Kent would agree with his recommendation to take formal action against Fullerton. Obviously, that was not a step to be taken lightly. And physicians had to be offered due process according to the medical staff bylaws.

Yet Aaron kept coming back to the potential impact to patient care. He wouldn't be able to live with himself if one of their small patients suffered because Fullerton didn't bother to answer his pages.

And waiting until they had a medical malpractice case hanging over their heads was not an option.

The following morning, Aaron made sure to get to the hospital early. For one thing, he wanted to check on Grace, but he also suspected Fullerton would show up early for their meeting.

He was right. At six forty, there was a knock at his door. Steeling himself for the upcoming unpleasant discussion, Aaron stood and opened the door.

Dale Fullerton was freshly showered, shaved, and dressed to kill in an expensive suit.

"You're early," Aaron said. "Rob Kent isn't here yet."

"I was hoping we could talk first without him," Fullerton said. "I think you're blowing this incident way out of proportion."

It wasn't just once incident, but he planned to wait until Rob Kent was there to go through everything. "Sorry, I have a few calls to make. You'll need to wait here for Rob." Aaron gestured to the pair of chairs off to the side of the outer office area. Normally, his receptionist would be there to help manage things, but Hannah didn't come in until seven thirty.

He hoped the meeting with Fullerton and Rob was over by then.

Maggie was right, he did not like conflict.

"I only need a few minutes," Fullerton insisted.

"Have a seat," Aaron said. "If my calls finish early, I'll let you know."

"But—" He didn't give Fullerton a chance to finish. Instead, he stepped back into his office and closed the door.

Just so that he wasn't lying, he made a few calls. One was to the seventh-south nursing station to see if Kyle was up there making rounds. The other was to the nurse at Grace's bedside in the PICU. Even though he'd checked in on the little girl, she had been scheduled to have a chest X-ray done.

"Yes, Dr. Monroe, the radiology tech has been here to take the X-ray," the nurse confirmed. "I'm sure the results will be available soon."

"Thank you." He hung up the phone, then logged into the patient medical record system. He took a few minutes to look at the chest X-ray for himself, more to buy time than anything.

Grace's lungs looked clear, and that meant she could be transferred out of the PICU to a regular floor later that morning. Satisfied Grace was on the mend, he logged off.

There were still five minutes to go before the meeting time, but when he heard deep male voices, he rose and came around to open his office door. Seeing Rob Kent brought a sense of relief.

The sooner he could get this meeting over with, the better.

"Rob. Dale. Please come in." He opened his door so the two physicians could enter. Fullerton's expression was earnest, as if he couldn't imagine why he'd been called to the principal's office.

Aaron was annoyed that Dale had put him in this position. If people would just do their jobs, the world would be a much better place.

"Thanks for agreeing to meet on short notice," Aaron said. He handed each physician a copy of the document he'd put together last night. "We're here to discuss Dale Fullerton's lack of answering pages and overall dereliction of duty."

"This is outrageous," Dale sputtered. But his eyes widened when he read the document Aaron had provided.

"I agree, your behavior is completely outrageous," Aaron said. "And I'm not willing to continue to jeopardize patient care by ignoring it."

"This is definitely a pattern of unacceptable behavior," Rob Kent said. The chief of staff turned to face Fullerton. "What do you have to say in response?"

Fullerton scowled but then sat back in his chair as if realizing he wasn't getting out of this meeting unscathed. "I'm going through some personal issues. I promise it won't happen again."

Aaron wanted to point out that he'd been going through personal issues, too, but managed to refrain. He didn't want either of these men to know about how upset he'd been since his own divorce.

He held Fullerton's gaze. "I can buy that excuse for one weekend, not four."

"You don't know what I'm going through," Fullerton snapped back.

"Maybe not, but that doesn't change the fact that patient care has been negatively impacted by your behavior," Rob Kent said in a calm voice. "I'm going to suspend you from duty for two weeks and order you to undergo counseling. You will not be allowed to return to work until I receive a report from your psychologist saying you're cleared for duty. And this will be the first step in the disciplinary action process. If after you return to work there's another incident where you neglect to answer your pages, we'll be having another more serious conversation."

Aaron was impressed with Kent's firm, decisive action. Based on the dazed expression on Fullerton's face, it was clearly a wake-up call. The message was to shape up or ship out.

He almost hoped Fullerton would leave rather than suffer the indignity of medical staff sanctions.

Fullerton shot to his feet. "Fine. Excuse me so I can make the appointment."

As he watched Fullerton leave, Aaron sighed, hoping he wouldn't have to deal with another situation like this again.

MAGGIE AWOKE Monday morning with an overwhelming sense of dread. This was it. The day the department of Child Protective Services would decide Joey's fate.

Running her fingers through her hair, she debated darting back to the hotel room she hadn't used since checking in to shower and change. Then she sighed and decided there was no point. There was no reason to dress to impress.

The chance of being approved as Joey's foster mother was slim to none.

She bowed her head, silently praying for God to ensure that Krista Monroe be granted the honor of becoming Joey's foster mother. At least that way she would be able to hang around for a while to help Joey transition to his new life.

Please, Lord Jesus, protect this little boy! Give him the loving family he deserves!

"Maggie? I hav'ta go to the bafroom." Joey rubbed his eyes sleepily. She rose from the cot and hurried over.

"You remember where it is, right?" She helped him down from the bed.

"Yeah." He looked down at his arms as if he'd forgotten he was no longer connected to tubes or wires. Then he looked up at her. "I'm hungry."

"We'll order breakfast after you use the bathroom," she promised. He was on a regular diet now, and the menu boasted several breakfast choices specifically for kids. Including Mickey Mouse pancakes and Pluto waffles.

Joey was finishing in the bathroom when she heard a raised voice in the hallway. "Sir? Where are you going?"

Instantly, Maggie shot to the doorway. She wasn't surprised to see Oliver Chism standing there, but his outward appearance was worse than ever. He was wearing the same clothes, sporting more stains, and his greasy hair stood up on end. He staggered down the hall, making a beeline for Joey's room.

She quickly stepped into the hallway and closed the door behind her. No way was he getting past her.

"I wanna see my kid!" Oliver's tone was loud and the words slightly slurred. Had he been drinking? She was about to ask, but as he grew closer, she noticed his pupils were dilated.

Drugs? She shot a glance at the nurse standing next to her. Her name tag read Sonja. "I need you to call security."

Sonja nodded and lifted a hand to an earpiece. "Security needed on seven south outside room 712."

"I wanna…" Oliver Chism stumbled and fell against the wall. He slumped there for a long moment, then his legs crumpled beneath him, and he slowly slid to the floor.

"Mr. Chism? Oliver?" Maggie eased forward, unsure if he was smart enough to play some sort of trick, pretending to need help only to jump up and attack her. She didn't trust the guy as far as she could throw him. But up close, she noticed his eyelids slid closed, and his mouth went slack.

What in the world? Had he overdosed on drugs?

"Call a medical emergency," Maggie said urgently. "Do you have Narcan up here?"

"Yes, but in pediatric doses." Sonja came to kneel beside her, her expression grave. "You think he overdosed?"

"I have no idea other than his pupils are dilated." To prove her point, Maggie pried open one eyelid. Oliver's pupil was so large she could barely see the brown of his iris around it. "Get as much Narcan as you can find and hurry. I don't know what he's taken or how much."

Sonja jumped to her feet and rushed off.

"Maggie? What's going on?" Aaron strode quickly down the hall toward her. He looked surprised to see Oliver Chism lying on the floor. "What happened to him?"

"Suspected drug overdose." She felt for his pulse. "We may have to start CPR."

"What about Narcan?" Aaron dropped to his knees beside her. She was keenly aware of his spicy aftershave wafting toward her.

"Sonja the nurse is getting it. She says they only have pediatric doses, though."

"We're going to need more than that," Aaron said. "We'll start with what she has on hand, then tell her to go to the next unit over to get more."

It was comforting to have Aaron there to share the crisis. Then the faint thready beat of Oliver's pulse beneath her fingertips vanished.

"No pulse. Starting CPR." She didn't hesitate to begin chest compressions. Sonja arrived a minute later holding nasal injectors in one hand.

"I have two milligrams of Narcan," she announced.

"Thanks. But we may need more. I'll give him these while you run to the next unit for additional doses," Aaron said.

Maggie continued to provide chest compressions as Aaron administered Narcan through nasal injection. She'd hoped the two milligrams would be enough to bring Oliver's pulse back.

Aaron finished giving the medication, then felt for Oliver's pulse. "Compressions are good, stop CPR."

She sat back on her heels, drawing in deep breaths to steady herself. It had been a long time since she'd had to give CPR. As an anesthesiologist, the goal was to never let a patient suffer a cardiac arrest while they were in the operating room.

And kids in general didn't need compressions very often.

"No pulse. I'll take over CPR," Aaron said.

"Let me." She couldn't explain why she was so determined to save Oliver Chism's life, but as much as she didn't want this guy to have custody of Joey, she also didn't want him to die right outside his son's room.

"I have another two milligrams of Narcan," Sonja said breathlessly, dropping the nasal doses on the floor next to Aaron. "I've called down to the pharmacy for more."

Maggie continued giving chest compressions as Aaron administered the additional Narcan. Adults could sometimes need up to six or eight milligrams, and they'd only given Oliver a total of four.

He was relatively skinny, though, so Maggie prayed the second two-milligram dose of Narcan would be enough.

More hospital staff gathered around them, but she didn't allow herself to be distracted. She stayed focused on providing the best chest compressions possible, circulating the Narcan Aaron had given to help counteract the drugs Oliver must have taken.

"Good pulse with CPR," Aaron said again. "Stop compressions. Let's see where we're at."

"We have an AED here too," someone said, gesturing to the automatic external defibrillator sitting on top of a red crash cart, "in case you need to shock him."

Aaron nodded, then rested his fingers against Oliver's neck to feel for his carotid. Then he smiled up at her. "He has a pulse. You did it."

"We did it." She sat back on her heels again, feeling the fine trickle of sweat rolling down her spine. "Let's get him connected to the AED."

In less than five minutes, they had Oliver connected to the portable heart monitor/defibrillator and had lifted him onto a gurney. Oliver groaned but didn't quite wake up. Maggie knew it would take time for the Narcan to counteract the drugs in his system and that he would likely need additional doses of Narcan too.

"We need to get him down to the emergency department ASAP," one of the residents said, "before he crashes again."

"Do you have more Narcan on that crash cart?" Aaron asked. "If so, take it with you."

"We do." Sonja pulled the medication from the drawer and dropped it onto the gurney. Moments later, Oliver disappeared into the elevator.

"Well, that was interesting." Maggie glanced at Aaron. "Good timing in showing up when you did."

"I wanted to be here when Kyle made rounds," he said with a wry smile. "You had the situation under control."

"I don't suppose we're able to use this incident against him when it comes to his fighting for custody." She frowned. "We don't know where he was when he took the drugs and I doubt he'll be arrested for suffering an overdose in the hospital."

"I think CPS needs to hear about this, but I guess it's up to them what they choose to do with that information." Aaron put his arm around her shoulder. "It's going to work out, you'll see."

"Yes, I know." She allowed herself a moment to lean against him. Once, she would have turned into his arms and kissed him. But that was before their divorce. "I'm sure you heard about Krista Monroe."

"Adam's wife?" Aaron looked confused. "I know I mentioned her earlier, but I thought you you wanted to be Joey's foster mother."

She flushed. "I did. But Krista came by yesterday. I assumed that was because you reached out to her. Anyway, as you pointed out Krista is already a foster parent, so I'm hoping that whoever takes Joey's case will agree to placing him with Krista and Adam."

"I see." Aaron's green gaze held hers. "And how do you feel about that?"

She flushed, surprised that Krista had approached Maggie of her own accord. "I think it's the best option for Joey. Krista said I could stay with them for a few days to ease his transition to a new home."

His gaze narrowed. "So you've given up the idea of moving here to become Joey's permanent foster mother."

Why did he look disappointed with her? Hadn't he been the one to warn her off heading down this path in the first place? She blew out an exasperated breath. "I don't see how that's any of your concern. Thanks for helping with Oliver Chism. I need to get back to Joey."

"Maggie," he started to say, but she lifted her hand to stop him.

"I don't want to argue with you anymore," she said, feeling incredibly weary. Most of that was the adrenaline crash from handling the medical emergency, but these interactions with Aaron only proved why they'd gotten divorced in the first place. "Please, Aaron. While I appreciate the support you've given Joey, it's time for you to leave me alone."

He looked taken aback by her comment, but that didn't stop her from slipping into Joey's room. The little boy had climbed up into the bed and was watching cartoons, completely oblivious as to what had just transpired in the hallway outside his room.

Maggie washed her hands in the bathroom, then sat beside Joey to order him a breakfast tray. She had a feeling the social worker would be here very soon.

And she wasn't giving up another second of the precious time she had left with the little boy.

CHAPTER TEN

Aaron called Officer Thomas to let him know that Oliver Chism was a patient after collapsing outside his son's room. Thomas agreed to meet him down in the emergency department where the medical staff was still working on him.

He and Maggie had done everything they could to save this guy, but in the darkest corner of his brain, he silently acknowledged that if Chism didn't make it, Maggie's life would be much easier. He and Maggie shared the Hippocratic oath of *do no harm*. Their quick response had hopefully saved Chism's life.

And if he had overdosed on drugs as he suspected based on his response to the Narcan doses, that should be enough for a judge to decide that Chism was not capable of caring for his son.

As he took the stairs down to the emergency department, he made a mental note to talk to Adam later. He hadn't realized his brother had passed along Maggie's desire to be a foster parent for Joey to his wife, Krista. And that Krista had taken it upon herself to find Maggie and Joey on seven south, offering her assistance in placing Joey in her care.

The part that bothered him was Maggie's apparent willingness to walk away from Joey, leaving the boy with Adam and Krista. From what he'd witnessed over the past three days, Maggie had been determined to take on the role as Joey's mother.

What had changed?

Disheartening to realize he still had trouble reading Maggie's feelings, much like when they were married. He shook off the troubling thoughts as he waded into the chaotic environment of the emergency department.

He found Oliver Chism's room without difficulty. To his surprise, the guy was awake but appeared groggy. As if he still had drugs in his system.

Aaron hovered in the doorway, hoping the team was aware of the possible rebound effect of a narcotic overdose. There had been cases where the Narcan wore off and the drugs still in the patient's system rebounded to previous levels.

Some patients didn't survive the second overdose.

When he saw the nurse hanging a Narcan drip, he realized there was no need to be concerned. The medical team were experts in pediatric care, not necessarily for adults, yet he was glad the doc at the bedside had the situation under control.

Despite his apparent overdose, Oliver Chism would not die here today.

"Dr. Aaron Monroe?" He turned to see a uniformed cop walking toward him. He recognized Officer Thomas from his earlier visit. "What's going on?"

"Thanks for coming." He gestured to the skinny guy

stretched out on the gurney. "I believe you know Oliver Chism."

Thomas's eyebrows shot up. "Yeah. What happened?"

"Maggie can probably tell you more than I can; she was standing outside the room when he showed up. I came upon them as he collapsed to the floor. His pupils were dilated, so we treated him as a narcotic drug overdose."

Thomas's expression turned grim. "Any idea what he took?"

"No, but I'm sure they'll run a tox screen." He nodded to the medical personnel in the room. "Maggie performed CPR while I administered the Narcan. The antidote worked; he started to come around after the second dose."

Thomas sighed. "There are days I wish I wasn't so good at my job. At least this latest stunt should prevent Chism from obtaining custody of Joey."

"I hope so, but that's why I wanted you to be aware of this latest incident." He scowled. "Especially since this is the second time Chism has shown up here at Children's Memorial. The previous attempt to see his son he mentioned having a lawyer."

"How did Chism get a family lawyer on the weekend?" Thomas asked.

"We suspect Chism has a personal injury lawyer; he mentioned getting money because of the truck that plowed into the bus, causing Joey to require surgery on top of losing his mother."

"Chism can probably recover some money on behalf of Joey," Thomas admitted. "But I would like to think the judge would find a way to make sure some of that money would be held for Joey's future, not for Chism to buy drugs."

He was no legal expert, but that sounded good to him. "Anything you can do to help with that would be great."

"When can I interview him?" Thomas asked, jutting his chin toward Chism.

"Let me check with the medical team." Aaron eased into the room, listening to the brief conversation between the nurse and the resident.

"His vitals are stable, but his pulse oximeter readings could be a little higher," the nurse said. Then she leaned in closer to her patient. "Mr. Chism, I need you to take a deep breath."

Chism's eyelids fluttered open, and he tried to do as the nurse asked. On the monitor over the patient's bedside, Aaron could see the pulse oximeter reading was hanging in the low eighties.

"Again," Aaron ordered in a strong, firm voice. "You need more oxygen going to your brain, so take another deep breath."

Chism did so, and his oxygen reading improved. The nurse shot him a look of exasperation, but then continued speaking to her patient. "Mr. Chism, I need you to keep taking deep breaths."

Chism nodded, his eyelids drifting closed.

He turned away and caught Officer Thomas's gaze. "Not sure he's in any condition to talk yet."

"I understand." Thomas glanced at his watch. "I can hang around here for a while."

"Great." He was relieved to hear Thomas wasn't giving up so easily. He was humbled by how people had stepped up to rally around Joey. "Would you like some coffee? I can get decent stuff from my office." He knew the emergency department had a coffeepot in the break room but figured it was old and stale by now.

"I'd appreciate that, thanks," Thomas said.

After brewing a cup of coffee from the machine in his office, he returned to the emergency department to hand the mug to Thomas. Then he debated the wisdom of heading back up to the seventh floor to talk to Maggie.

If his ex-wife really was heading back to Boston soon, he couldn't wait any longer to talk to her. Ever since they'd responded to the bus crash, their conversations had been interrupted. His work, mostly, he was forced to acknowledge.

He frowned, remembering how she'd told him to go ahead and take the call because patient care was a priority. Words she'd said many times before.

But for the first time it occurred to him that her saying the words didn't mean he should have responded the way he had. Why hadn't he made their marriage a higher priority? It wasn't as if physicians could ignore their patients, but he tended to keep a close eye on the care provided by the residents.

Some might even accuse him of micromanaging them.

This weekend, he shouldn't have been on call in the first place, but he had ended up responding to calls and taking Grace to surgery. Yet now that he was looking back, he realized he could have asked another colleague to help cover Fullerton's case.

But he hadn't. In truth, the thought hadn't even occurred to him.

He turned and headed back to his office, feeling sick with the realization that he owned a bigger piece of their failed marriage than he'd previously accepted.

And worse, he was pretty sure that it was too late to do anything about it.

"MS. DALL?" A petite blonde poked her head into Joey's room. "I'm Rochelle, the social worker for this unit."

Maggie glanced at Joey who was once again engrossed with the television. She moved toward the doorway, not sure it was smart to have this conversation in front of the little boy. "Please call me Maggie," she said with a smile. "Is there someplace we can talk?"

"Ah, sure. Let's go down to the lounge." Rochelle led the way down the hall. "I understand Joey's father has tried to see him a few times."

"Yes." Maggie dropped into the open seat beside Rochelle. "Unfortunately, he collapsed in the hallway. Dr. Aaron Monroe and I initiated CPR and emergency treatment for what we suspected was a narcotic overdose."

"Yes, I heard all about it from Tina, Joey's nurse," Rochelle said. "I just checked with the emergency department social worker; Luanne has informed me that Mr. Chism's condition has been stabilized."

"That's good to hear." Maggie had wondered how Oliver Chism was doing. It had taken so much Narcan to reverse the effects of whatever drugs he'd ingested, so she knew the outcome could have been much different.

"He owes his life to you and Dr. Monroe," Rochelle said.

Maggie shrugged. "Anyone else would have done the same. I just happened to be the closest provider." She didn't add that the main reason she'd been standing there in the first place was to make sure Chism didn't get anywhere near his son.

"Well, you did great work." Rochelle glanced at the

tablet on her lap. "As you know, Joey's mother passed away in the bus crash."

"Yes, I was there. Aaron—er—Dr. Monroe tried to save her life." Maggie remembered how he'd called the code after several rounds of CPR and shocking Joey's mother hadn't worked.

"I see. I also understand you've stayed at Joey's side since the accident," Rochelle continued. "The nursing staff have been very impressed with your dedication to Joey."

"Again, I happened to be the person Joey latched onto." Maggie knew that if someone else had gone into the bus with Aaron, she wouldn't be sitting there. "Once I took him from his mother's arms, he wouldn't let me go."

"One of the Children's Memorial nurses, a Krista Monroe—wait, is she a relation to Dr. Monroe?" Rochelle asked, interrupting herself.

"Yes, she's married to Adam Monroe, who is a pediatrician on staff. Adam and Aaron are brothers." The two eldest Monroe sons also looked very much alike, although in her humble opinion, Aaron was more handsome.

"Very interesting. That information certainly helps her case," Rochelle said as she made a note on her tablet. "I received word that Krista Monroe is requesting Joey be placed with her and her husband on a temporary basis. I'm not sure how familiar you are with the family court system, but it will take time to work through temporary and permanent guardianship."

So far, Rochelle wasn't telling Maggie anything she didn't already know. "Mr. Chism, Joey's father, has made it clear he would like to have custody of his son." Maggie forced the statement past her tight throat. "He made that statement again, shortly before he collapsed in the hallway outside his son's room."

"I see." Rochelle's expression turned grim. "Well, if he overdosed on drugs, he'll need to prove he's clean before the judge will consider him as a viable guardian."

"Clean for how long?" Maggie asked, battling a wave of anger. "He overdosed here at the hospital. Surely that proves he's not fit to take care of a four-year-old child."

"That's true, but Oliver Chism has the right to prove he's capable of getting clean." Rochelle's smile was sad. "Even if that takes six months to a year, the judge will be willing to hear the case once he's completed a stint in rehab."

Maggie tried not to let her frustration show. Logically, she knew that Rochelle was only being honest about a foster family getting custody long term, but the thought of Oliver Chism taking Joey home even a year from now, only to fall off the wagon to the point he might overdose in front of his own son, was horrifying.

She linked her fingers together in her lap. "I know it's probably too soon, but I completed the online application to be a foster parent too. I did that specifically for Joey, as we've bonded over the weekend."

"Really?" Rochelle looked surprised. "I only heard about Krista Monroe, nothing about your application. I can check into that for you, but the process of becoming a foster parent takes time. It's rarely approved any quicker than six weeks."

Tears pricked Maggie's eyes, but she brushed them away. "I understand. I just hoped that for Joey's sake..." What could she say? That she'd hoped being an anesthesiologist would send her application to the top of the pile? That she believed she was more qualified than any of the other foster parents out there?

Not just because of her medical background but because she already loved the little boy like a son?

"Ms. Dall, I can appreciate how you feel," Rochelle said gently. "I'll mention your application to the caseworker, but in my humble opinion, Krista and Adam Monroe have a better chance of getting emergency placement for Joey. Especially since they both have medical background and can deal with his recent surgery."

She hadn't corrected Rochelle in using the title of Ms. instead of Dr., but it was tempting. "I'm a physician too," she said. "But I understand what you're saying. I will, of course, abide by the CPS caseworker's decision of where to place Joey after his discharge."

"Great." Rochelle looked relieved.

"Maggie! Maggie!" Hearing her name, Maggie jumped to her feet and ran out of the lounge toward Joey's room. She barreled inside, her heart wrenching when she found him sobbing. "I thought you left me."

"No, Joey, I'm here." She gathered him close. "I'm sorry I was gone longer than I expected."

He wrapped his arms tightly around her neck. "You'll stay wif me, right?"

"Yes, Joey. I'm staying." She couldn't bring herself to let him know that he'd be going home with someone else. Thankfully, Krista had agreed she could accompany the little boy to help him make the transition.

But for how long? That was the most important question. She didn't care how much of her vacation time she'd have to burn or how many favors she'd need to call upon to help cover her shifts.

But even as that thought formed in her mind, it dawned on her that Joey might not accept Krista's role in his life as long as Maggie was there to comfort him. He'd keep leaning on her rather than establishing new bonds.

She pressed a kiss to the top of Joey's head, deciding she needed input from the child psychologist now more than ever. The little boy's hysterical meltdown at being left alone reminded her of post-traumatic stress syndrome.

Something no child should have to suffer.

Then again, as much as Joey had lost, other kids suffered worse at the hands of their parents or guardians. Closing her eyes, she lifted her heart in prayer.

Please, Lord Jesus, keep Joey safe in Your care. Let Thy will be done. Amen.

Joey relaxed against her. She rocked him back and forth, murmuring words of comfort. After fifteen minutes, he turned his head so that he could continue to watch the children's movie that was playing on the screen. Another one she'd never seen before. Then again, other than caring for kids in a hospital setting, she hadn't cared for them at home.

No doubt, she had a lot to learn.

She consoled herself with the thought that most new parents had to learn the best way to handle taking care of their kids too. No child came with an instruction manual.

"Maggie?" She glanced over to see Aaron standing in the doorway.

"Hi." She had expected him to show up sooner or later. "I heard Chism's condition has been stabilized."

"Yep." Aaron moved into the room, his green gaze softening at the sight of Joey snuggled in her arms. "I hate to bother you, but he wants to talk to you."

"Who? Chism?" She frowned. "Why on earth would he want that?"

Aaron shrugged. "Not sure. But I told Officer Thomas I'd come up to ask if you'd mind going down to see him."

When she didn't immediately answer, he added, "It's up to you, but I think it's worth it to hear what the guy has to say."

"You do?" She shook her head. "I don't know if that's a smart idea."

"I doubt he'll be disrespectful with Officer Thomas hovering nearby," Aaron said.

"He's not the one I'm worried about." She held his gaze for a long moment. "I may say something I'll regret. Well, to be honest, I wouldn't regret it, but my comments might come back to haunt me."

The corner of Aaron's mouth kicked up in a smile. "I share your sentiments, but I'll make sure no one records the conversation."

She glanced down at Joey, loathe to disturb him. But a sense of obligation nagged at her. "Joey, will you be okay here if I have to run downstairs for a few minutes?" She smoothed his hair away from his forehead. "I won't be gone long, and I'll come right back here when I'm finished."

Joey lifted his head to look at her. "You won't leave without me?"

She knew he was afraid she'd leave him alone in the hospital. "I promise I won't leave without you."

He nodded slowly. "Okay. I'll watch my show while you're gone."

"Thank you." She eased from his bed, straightening her badly wrinkled clothes. "I'll be back as soon as possible."

"Have you eaten breakfast?" Aaron asked. "I can grab something for you if needed."

"There hasn't been time for me to eat," she admitted. She hoped he hadn't heard her stomach growling. She hadn't felt right accepting a free parent tray from the kitchen as she technically wasn't Joey's legal guardian. "I'll swing by the cafeteria on my way back up to Joey's room."

"Did you hear that, Joey? Maggie needs to stop and get breakfast too," Aaron said. "She'll be back very soon."

Joey nodded. "Okay."

Maggie frowned as she followed Aaron down the hall toward the elevator. "I hope I don't miss the child psychologist."

"I hope not, too, but if so, we can ask the doc to swing by again." He pushed the button to summon the car. "You need to eat, and this meeting with Chism shouldn't take too long."

"Did you call Officer Thomas?" she asked as they rode down to the emergency department.

"Oh yeah. I wanted him to know what happened." Aaron shook his head. "I really hope the court doesn't give Chism custody of Joey."

"I hope not too." She remembered the layout of the emergency department from those hours she spent holding Joey. Finding Oliver Chism's room wasn't difficult, and Officer Thomas gave her a nod when they walked in.

"Dr. Dall. Thanks for stopping down." Thomas looked toward Oliver. "Mr. Chism, you remember Dr. Maggie Dall."

"Yeah." Chism shifted on the bed. She stepped closer, raking her gaze over the monitor readings. He played with the pulse oximeter on his finger, then lifted his head to flash her a chagrined look. "I heard you saved my life."

She nodded slowly. "You almost died."

"I know." He put a hand to his chest, and she wondered if her chest compressions had cracked a couple of his ribs. That was always a possibility, even if they were done correctly. "The doc said if you hadn't been there, I woulda died."

That was probably stretching the truth, as anyone could

have done CPR. However, she decided not to quibble. "But I was there, and you survived. That's what's important."

"I want you to have custody of Joey," he said. "I know I got problems, and I can't take care of my boy. I want you to be the one to take care of him."

Stunned, she wasn't sure what to say. As touching as Oliver Chism's statement was, the situation was more complicated than he seemed to understand.

A parent couldn't just hand over their child to another adult. But she was glad Oliver wouldn't stand in the way of Joey being placed with a foster care family he deserved.

Maybe this was God's way of answering her prayers.

CHAPTER ELEVEN

Aaron stared at Oliver Chism, amazed that the guy's near-death experience had caused him to accept his limitations as a father.

At least for now. He wasn't so sure the guy wouldn't change his mind at some point and file again for custody.

"I would like nothing better than to take care of your son, but that's not how the system works," Maggie said.

Chism scowled. "But that's what I want. Don't I get a vote as the boy's father?"

Maggie glanced helplessly at Aaron. He had no idea what to say. This was all outside his realm of experience, but he suspected that CPS wasn't going to simply give in to the wishes of a biological father with drug addiction issues.

"I'm not sure that's within Dr. Dall's purview," Officer Thomas said.

She flashed Thomas a grateful look, then turned back to Oliver. "I will speak with the representative from Child Protective Services," she said. "If nothing else, I will do my best to ensure Joey is placed with a wonderful foster family."

"But—that's not what I want!" Chism was growing agitated now, the monitor over his bedside beeping as his oxygen percentage plummeted.

"Mr. Chism, please, you need to relax." Maggie put a hand on Oliver's arm. "I will do my best, okay? I don't have control over what the department decides."

"Okay." Chism pressed his hand to his chest. "I don't feel so good."

"Please follow the doctor's orders," Maggie said. "And you must know you need to find a way to get clean."

Chism flushed and nodded. "I know I do."

Aaron stepped forward. "We're working on getting Mr. Chism transferred to Trinity Medical Center," he said. "They are better equipped to handle adults with medical concerns."

"Great." Maggie managed a smile.

"Take care of Joey," Chism said as Maggie turned to leave.

"I will." She nodded at Officer Thomas and edged past Aaron, who followed her back through the emergency department. "That was rather unexpected," she said when they were out of Oliver Chism's earshot.

"Yeah, surprised me too," he agreed. "I don't know how much weight CPS will give to his request, though."

"Probably not much," she said with a sigh. "I can't imagine they'll look highly on a man who thinks you can hand over your kid like you do a car."

"But if they did take his wishes into consideration, you'd willingly step in to care for Joey, right?"

"Yes." She answered without hesitation. "I would love nothing more."

They paused outside the bank of elevators. "Then why didn't you want to adopt a child with me?"

"What?" She turned to stare at him. "Oh, you mean the offhand comment you made about looking into adoption while you were texting with the residents about one of your patients? That wasn't exactly a conversation, Aaron. It was more like you couldn't have cared less about what I was going through."

It was his turn to be shocked. "What do you mean? I cared about what you were going through."

She scoffed. "You never said you were sorry to hear the results of my fertility testing. You didn't seem to notice I was grieving. Your attention was centered on the patient you were texting about, not me. Us. Or our future as a family."

Had he really done that? Made her feel as if he didn't care? He winced as he remembered she'd broached the subject of her final testing results after a particularly difficult surgery he'd performed earlier that day. So yeah, he probably had been distracted. But that didn't mean he didn't care.

"Never mind," Maggie said, turning away. "There's no point in rehashing our past."

He reached out to grasp her arm. "Maggie, I'm sorry, but that wasn't my intent. Of course, I knew you were grieving, but we talked about your testing. We discussed what the likely results would be. I guess I wasn't surprised by the news and was already thinking ahead to our next steps. So yes, I mentioned adoption. I didn't mean it to sound casual or offhand. I meant it when I suggested we go through the process."

She eyed him thoughtfully. "Do you have any idea what the process is like? It's not like you fill out a form and a baby gets dropped into your lap. You would have had to take time off work, Aaron. *Uninterrupted time off work*," she said with emphasis. "Something you couldn't manage even on our honeymoon."

"We had a great honeymoon." Or so he'd thought. "I only took a couple of calls; we spent an entire week in Paris like you wanted."

"Paris was lovely, and you're a good guy. But you took more than a couple calls, Aaron. There was one day you were on the phone for almost an hour straight."

He nodded slowly, remembering the calls about a patient he'd cared for that had gotten readmitted with an infection. "Okay, you're right. I did take calls. But we still had a wonderful time." He paused, then added, "Didn't we?"

"We did, but only because I didn't make a big deal out of the calls you had with your colleagues." She sighed. "When you made that comment about adopting, I guess I got angry. There you were texting away while I was reeling from the news that I would never have a baby. Our baby."

The elevator dinged. The doors opened, and several staff members stepped off, going around them. Aaron realized this wasn't the place to have this conversation. But he also knew that he couldn't just let her walk away. Maybe he'd made mistakes, but Maggie hadn't told him any of this when she'd filed for divorce.

"We need to talk about this, Maggie," he said in a low tone. "We should have talked this through two years ago."

"What's the point?" She shrugged. "You can't change who you are, Aaron. Look at you, Chairman of Pediatric Cardiac Surgery! That's even more responsibility than you had back in Boston. You're a born leader, and I get that." She pulled from his grasp to jump into the elevator. "I need to get back to Joey."

He quickly stepped through the closing doors, causing them to abruptly reopen. "I'm coming with you."

She shot him an exasperated look. "There's no reason for you to sit at Joey's bedside."

He knew what she was really saying. Their conversation was over. They were not getting back together anytime soon.

But he didn't agree. Obviously having a heart-to-heart talk in front of Joey wasn't possible. There had to be another way to bridge the gap between them.

Then his pager went off. He felt Maggie's gaze boring into him as he pulled the device from his belt.

"Go ahead, Aaron. I understand. You're working." She wasn't being snarky, but a hint of resignation laced her tone. "I'm surprised you're not in the OR today."

"I have two cases tomorrow." He clipped the pager back onto his belt, trying to find a way to salvage this. He'd have to answer the resident soon, but that call could wait a few minutes. They reached the seventh floor, and as the elevator doors opened, he felt the moment slipping away. "Maggie, will you have lunch with me?" He frowned. "You forgot to swing by the cafeteria to grab breakfast."

"I'll do that later." She waved off his concern. "And no, Aaron, I don't think there's a reason for us to have lunch together while you're working."

"Maggie, wait..." But it was no use. She was striding purposefully down the hall toward Joey's room. And his pager went off again anyway.

She was right, lunch while he was working was a bad idea. If he wanted to continue to have a heartfelt conversation with Maggie, he needed to find a way to spend time with her when he wasn't bombarded by calls and pagers.

But how? As he turned away to reach for his phone, he tried to come up with a viable solution.

One that would convince Maggie to give him another chance.

MAGGIE TRIED to squash the flash of guilt that washed over her as she walked away from Aaron for the second time. If she were being honest, the shock and confusion in his eyes over how things had ended between them made her feel as if she'd been in the wrong.

Had she? It seemed so obvious to her back then that Aaron wasn't seriously considering adoption, that he'd tossed that out there as a way to make her feel better, while being preoccupied with his patient situation, but maybe she had read into his comments.

Putting a negative spin on them.

Still, that didn't change the fact that she could not give him the next generation of Monroe children. And she had felt certain he'd have moved on by now, finding someone who would be able to give him the children he wanted.

So why hadn't he?

Because of his job, most likely. When they'd first met, she'd admired his dedication to his patients. He was still a phenomenal and skilled surgeon. It wasn't that she wanted to take that away from him.

But there had to be more to life than a career. Even Aaron had mentioned how his parents had made things work over the years. She enjoyed being an anesthesiologist, but her work was different in that her responsibility started in the pre-op area, through the procedure, and then for the following recovery phase in the PACU. Once she went home, she was rarely called back to deal with a problem.

Shaking off the thoughts, she considered grabbing a couple of crackers from the kitchen to ease the rumbling in her stomach. Then she spied a woman dressed in an ill-fitting black suit approaching from the other end of the hall.

They met outside Joey's room. Her visitor's name tag read Francis Douglas, but Maggie also saw her state issued ID clipped to the other collar.

Francis Douglas was from the Department of Health and Human Services.

"Hello. I'm Dr. Maggie Dall." She extended her hand to the woman. "I have been staying with Joey since the bus crash."

"Dr. Dall, I'm social worker Francis Douglas," the woman responded, giving her hand a firm shake. "I have heard a lot about you."

Good or bad? The thought flitted through Maggie's mind, but she didn't voice it. "If you don't mind, I need to let Joey know I'm back. Then we can talk."

"Actually, I'm here to talk to Joey," Francis said.

Maggie winced at her blunder. Of course, this woman wasn't there just to talk to Maggie. She managed to keep her smile in place as she entered the room.

"You're back," Joey said, looking relieved. "You were gone a long time."

"Sorry about that." She crossed over to his bedside. "This is Ms. Douglas. She wants to talk to you, okay?"

"I'm watching *Cars*," Joey protested, barely giving Francis Douglas a glance. "It's a really good movie."

"Joey, you can watch that when you're finished." She put a note of steel in her tone. "This is important."

"But—" Joey started to argue, but she reached over and

turned off the television. He scowled. "Hey! I wanna watch!"

"We can watch the movie later," she reiterated, ignoring his mulish expression. "Don't argue with me, Joey. We need to speak with Ms. Douglas now."

"Actually, Dr. Dall, if you don't mind, I'd like to speak with Joey alone," the caseworker said.

She hadn't expected that but realized she should have. "Oh, yes. I understand. I'll run and get something to eat."

"Great." Ms. Douglas turned to Joey. "My name is Francis. I'd like to ask you a few questions."

"Okay." Now Joey looked nervous, glancing toward Maggie as if for reassurance.

She smiled and nodded. "Go ahead, Joey. You're not in any trouble. Be honest when you're speaking with Ms. Douglas, okay? Everything will work out just fine. I'll be back in a little while." It took every ounce of willpower Maggie had to turn and leave the room.

In the hallway, she hesitated, tempted to linger outside the room and listen in. Then she realized she was being foolish. She didn't have anything to fear from Joey speaking with the caseworker.

But she was concerned about the little boy having to relive those moments he lost his mother in the bus crash. What if he started crying again?

Maybe she wasn't giving Francis Douglas enough credit. Her job was to deal with traumatized kids. She would be gentle with Joey.

Her stomach chose that moment to rumble with hunger, making her realize crackers weren't going to cut it. She needed real food. Preferably something with protein. She turned and headed back toward the bank of elevators. It wouldn't take long to grab something to eat, the way she'd intended to do earlier.

Before she'd gotten sidetracked by Aaron.

She'd been surprised when he'd asked her to lunch. He'd almost looked as if he'd missed her as much as she missed him.

But that didn't mean they could pick up the fractured pieces of their marriage, putting them back together again.

Yet she was a little surprised how much she wanted to.

Enough. She strode into the cafeteria, heading to the breakfast offerings. She decided to pick up a breakfast sandwich like she had yesterday. It was fast and easy, compared to waiting in line for an omelet.

As she left the cafeteria, she paused when she saw Aaron standing off to the side speaking with another staff member. Aaron was scowling, as if he was not happy with how the conversation was going. He was so focused on the discussion he didn't see her.

"You're going to regret this." The man speaking harshly had his back to Maggie, so she couldn't see his face. But she could see the back of his neck was bright red with anger or embarrassment.

Maybe both.

"You brought this on yourself, Dale. I had to cover your call this weekend, remember?" Aaron's voice was reasonable, but there was no mistaking the anger in his eyes. "Walk away before I have to take more action against you."

"Oh, you'd like that, wouldn't you?" Dale sneered.

"No, actually, I wouldn't," Aaron said, looking tired. "Walk. Away. Now."

Maggie had stopped in the middle of the hall, half afraid she'd have to break up an altercation between them.

Thankfully, Dale must have realized they had an audience. He abruptly turned, shot her a look of pure venom, and stalked off.

Aaron hung his head for a moment, then seemed to notice her. "Hey. Glad you decided to get something to eat."

She glanced at her almost forgotten sandwich, then shrugged. "Yes, the caseworker from CPS is upstairs with Joey. She wanted to speak to him alone, without me."

Aaron frowned. "Is that normal?"

"No clue." She gestured to the man stalking down the hall in the opposite direction. "Who was that guy? Why is he so angry with you?"

"Dale Fullerton, and he's ticked because I forced the issue of his not answering calls and pages on the weekends." He came closer. "What do you think the caseworker is asking Joey? Will she make a decision today regarding temporary foster placement?"

"I imagine she has to decide that since it looks to me like Joey is stable enough for discharge." She was a little surprised by the concern on Aaron's features. He clearly cared about Joey's future as much as she did.

Again, she couldn't help feeling as if she'd treated him badly. As if she were just as responsible for the breakup of their marriage as she'd believed him to be. Sure, she'd thought she was being noble by leaving so he could have the family he deserved, but maybe she'd been fooling herself.

Telling herself their divorce was more Aaron's fault than hers.

"The suspense is killing me. Let's head up and see what she's decided." Aaron placed his hand on the small of her back. "But a bit of friendly advice? You should eat that egg and cheese bagel before it gets cold. I can attest to the fact that cold breakfast sandwiches are not very good."

She chuckled and unwrapped one corner of the sandwich to take a bite. Mostly because she was too hungry not to. "I almost stayed out in the hall to listen to their conversation," she confided as they headed up to the seventh floor. Riding on the elevator with Aaron was becoming a habit.

"I would have done that too," he admitted. "But you know how much Joey cares about you. I'm sure he'll make his feelings clear to the caseworker."

She was touched by how he was trying to reassure her. "Thanks, but I don't think Ms. Douglas is going to be swayed by Joey's telling her how much he likes me."

"And why not?" Aaron asked with exasperation "After all, Joey's opinion should matter the most. That poor kid has been through a lot, losing his mother, then having surgery. The kid deserves a vote regarding his future."

"That's sweet of you to say." She took another bite of her breakfast sandwich as the poky elevator seemed to stop on every floor. "As much as I want to be there for him, I've been praying Joey gets placed with Krista and Adam. As you pointed out, I don't even live in Wisconsin anymore. I highly doubt I'll be considered a viable option to step in as Joey's foster mother."

"You're an excellent anesthesiologist," Aaron said firmly. "Successful and more than capable of providing for Joey's emotional and financial needs. More so than anyone else, if you ask me. Even his own father wants you to care for him."

"A drug addict father," she said. "Not sure that matters much either."

"Well, maybe not, but at least he thanked you for saving his life," Aaron said.

They stepped off the elevator and headed toward Joey's room. When Maggie heard Joey's sobs, she broke into a run.

Seconds later, she burst into the room. "What is it? What's wrong?"

"Maggie!" Joey practically threw himself into her arms. He wrapped his arms tightly around her neck, almost to the point she couldn't breathe. "I don't wanna go away wif someone else. I want you!"

"Shh, it's okay. Don't worry, everything is going to be okay." She dropped the remains of her breakfast sandwich on the table and cradled the little boy close, her worst fears seeming to materialize in front of her eyes.

From the stern expression on Francis Douglas's face, it appeared the CPS caseworker had already made up her mind about where Joey was going to live.

And it wasn't with her or Krista and Adam.

CHAPTER TWELVE

Hovering in the doorway to Joey's room, Adam's heart squeezed at how the little boy clung to Maggie. Glancing at the caseworker, he realized she was frowning.

What did she expect from a traumatized child? Of course, he's going to seek comfort and support from the one consistent adult who had been there for him since he'd tragically lost his mother.

"Please, Ms. Douglas," Maggie said. "Please consider placing Joey with Krista and Adam Monroe. I know Krista, and she will allow me to help Joey transition into his new home."

"Don't wanna," Joey muttered against her neck.

"But I'll be with you at Krista and Adam's house." Maggie smoothed a hand down the child's back.

Joey lifted his head, his gaze hopeful. "You will?"

"Yes." Maggie shot a quick glance at the caseworker who hadn't said anything yet. "I will stay with you for as long as you need me."

Ms. Douglas's frown deepened. "I'm not sure that will be in Joseph's best interest."

Maggie looked as if she might cry. Aaron took a step into the room. "It might be best to check with the child psychologist on staff to get a professional opinion on that. After all, Joey has been through several traumatic events. A little stability would likely help him cope."

Ms. Douglas turned to look at him. "Who are you?"

"Dr. Aaron Monroe. Adam is my brother and a pediatrician as well." Aaron couldn't imagine a better placement for Joey than with his brother and Krista. "And his wife, Krista, is a pediatric nurse. Do you really have any other foster families more qualified to care for this child? I understand there's a severe shortage of foster parents out there. I'd like to think you'd jump on the chance my brother and his wife are offering."

The caseworker sighed. "Okay, I will see what we can do about placing Joey with Krista and Adam Monroe."

"Thank you," Maggie said. "And if you could ask your supervisor to review my application, too, I would be grateful. I would like to take Joey in on a permanent basis."

"I'll make a note of that too." Ms. Douglas didn't seem overly happy, but her gaze softened when she looked at Joey. "He does seem content with you."

"Yes, he is." Maggie's smile lit up her face. "Thank you so much. I promise to take excellent care of Joey."

"I would like to see the child psychologist's report, though," Ms. Douglas said.

"Of course." Maggie glanced up at the clock on the way. "I asked for a referral yesterday, but obviously, I don't know how many patients they need to see. If someone doesn't swing by soon, I'll ask the nurse to page the psychologist on duty."

"As a physician, you understand how the system works," Ms. Douglas said.

"Yes, I do." Maggie looked determined. "And that's why I think I'm the best option for Joey."

"It's nice to know Krista and Adam Monroe have already been approved. That should make things easier." The caseworker turned to leave. "I'll be in touch soon," she said over her shoulder.

"I don't like her," Joey said. "She's mean."

"She's not mean, she's doing her job, and it's not a very easy one. You need to treat her nicely," Maggie admonished. "I don't want to hear you say anything bad about her."

Joey ducked his head. "Okay."

Aaron fought the urge to smile. Watching Maggie and Joey only reinforced what he'd always known. Maggie would be a wonderful mother. To Joey and other children too.

And he very much wanted to be her partner in that endeavor.

"Maggie, would you please have dinner with me?" She'd refused his offer to have lunch together, but he was determined not to let her go without a fight.

The way he should have fought for her prior to their divorce.

"I'm not sure what time Joey will be discharged or if he'll really get to go to Krista and Adam's home." Her gaze clung to his for a long moment. "I'll probably need to stay close to Joey."

"I understand." He tucked his hands into the pockets of his lab coat. "I'll check back with you later. If Joey does get discharged to Krista and Adam's, maybe I can bring dinner to you."

She tilted her head to the side, eyeing him curiously. "Are you sure?"

"Yes." He looked at the little boy. "Joey, do you like spaghetti?"

Joey nodded. "Meatballs!"

"I like spaghetti and meatballs too," he assured the boy. "How about if I bring that over for dinner later?"

Joey nodded, then glanced up at the television. "Can I watch my movie now?"

"Of course." Maggie settled the boy back in his hospital bed. She lifted the edge of his gown to double-check his incision, then smiled. "I'll restart the movie *Cars* for you."

"Goodie," Joey said, reclining on the pillows.

Maggie played with the controls, then moved toward him. "Let me guess, takeout spaghetti and meatballs?"

"Yep, from Giovani's," he said with a smile. "Better than anything I can make."

"Oh, I'm well aware of your lack of cooking skills," she said dryly. "Nice of you to offer to bring dinner."

"Maggie, I'd really like some time to talk." He had to restrain himself from reaching out to draw her into his arms. "I know I made some mistakes, but I don't think I'm solely responsible for our breakup."

He half expected her to argue, but she nodded thoughtfully. "No, you're right in that we both share that responsibility." She tucked a wayward curl behind her ear. "I'd like to make sure Joey is settled in before leaving him, though."

"I know, that's why I figured I'd bring dinner. Maybe after he falls asleep?" Hope swelled in his heart. "I'll wait as long as it takes."

"Okay." She managed a smile. "I'll let you know if anything changes with Joey's condition or his discharge plan."

"Great." He wished he could kiss her but settled for returning her smile. "I'll see you and Joey soon."

As if reading his mind, she leaned in to give him a quick kiss on the cheek. "Thanks for your support with Ms. Douglas."

"Anytime." He had to force himself to turn away. "Later, then."

"Later." He sensed her watching him as he left the room. Reaching for his phone, he called his brother Adam to fill him in on the plan. Adam didn't answer, likely seeing patients, so Aaron sent a quick text indicating Adam should call him.

Thirty minutes passed before Adam returned his call. Aaron was back in his office after checking in on Grace. "I just heard from Krista. Sounds like Joey is coming home with us and your ex-wife."

"For sure? Krista heard that from CPS?" Aaron asked.

"Yes, less than five minutes ago," Adam said. "We're thrilled, but I know Maggie is the one Joey has bonded with."

Aaron winced. "I know, and I'm sure that will make things difficult for you and Krista. I mean, I know how badly you want a family of your own."

"We do," Adam said. "But that's the thing. Krista took a pregnancy test earlier this morning, and it's positive." His brother sounded thrilled. "We're going to have a baby in roughly seven months."

"That's wonderful news," Aaron said, even as he felt a strange twinge in the region of his heart. Once he'd hoped to hear those words from Maggie.

But maybe it was time to accept that God had other plans for them.

"Thanks, we're thrilled. And hopefully, Maggie's application will get approved too," Adam said. "It sounds like she really wants to care for Joey."

That was putting it mildly. "She does."

"We'll pray for the two of them to stay together," Adam said. The sound of a baby crying came through the phone's speaker. "That's my cue. I have to go; my next patient is here."

"One more thing, I'm bringing dinner tonight from Giovani's," Aaron said quickly. "You and Krista won't need to do anything."

"Great, I'll let her know. Bye." Adam disconnected from the call.

Aaron sat back in his desk chair for a moment, then fired off a couple of emails to make sure he was not on call for the evening. Then he glanced up at the ceiling. He couldn't see the sky overhead, but that was okay. He knew God was up there looking down at him.

Drawing in a deep breath, he closed his eyes and prayed. *Please, Lord, grant me the wisdom to make things right with Maggie! Amen.*

THE REST of the day passed quicker than Maggie could have imagined. Kyle Flores dropped in to see Joey. After a thorough exam, Kyle declared him medically stable for discharge. The child psychologist came through as well, spending a solid forty-five minutes with Joey. Maggie was impressed by how Dr. Starland asked probing questions and managed to get key information from the little boy.

Like the fact that his mother was taking him to get food the day of the bus crash.

From what Maggie gathered, Pamela was barely scraping by. Joey said they didn't always have milk for his cereal in the morning. And that he usually had a half of a peanut butter and jelly sandwich for lunch because he and his mom shared it. The more she listened to the child, the more she was irked by how Joey's father hadn't provided any financial support.

Yet she was humbled by how much Pamela seemed to care for Joey, traveling by bus to various food pantries to obtain badly needed groceries. From what Joey described, a longer bus trip offered the best items.

"One time, we got a bag of mini chocolate chip cookies there!" His eyes gleamed with excitement. "That was my favorite."

Maggie made a mental note to provide a financial donation to the food pantries in the city in honor of Joey's mom.

When the psychologist was finished, Maggie followed her out of the room. "A Ms. Francis Douglas from Child Protective Services would like a copy of your report on Joey. I've applied to be a foster parent, but there's another couple, Krista and Adam Monroe, who are already approved as foster parents, and I've requested Joey be placed with them so that I can be there to help with the transition."

"I saw the note from the social worker related to his situation," Dr. Starland said. "I think Joey is doing remarkably well considering the trauma he's been through. It's obvious he's become very attached to you. He's viewing you as his surrogate mother, the woman keeping him safe now that his mother isn't there to do that for him. My professional opinion supports keeping you involved in his care as much as possible, and I'll be happy to add that to my report."

Tears of gratitude pricked Maggie's eyes, and it was all she could do not to throw her arms around the woman. "That would be wonderful. Thank you."

"He's a bright and well-adjusted little boy," Dr. Starland said. "Much of that is thanks to you choosing to be there for him. I'm not so sure anyone else would have done the same."

"I'm sure they would if they could," Maggie said. "Thankfully, I was able to get off work to stay with him." She understood her role as an anesthesiologist gave her a privilege many others couldn't afford. She could use her vacation time and had plenty of money saved up for additional expenses she might have. And she had a career that enabled her to relocate to Milwaukee without difficulty. Most health systems were hiring, and she was confident she'd be able to secure another position.

Most people, especially those outside the medical field didn't have that flexibility.

"I'm glad." Dr. Starland patted her arm. "It was nice to meet you."

"You too." Maggie turned to head back inside Joey's room. Now that things were moving in the right direction, it was time to clear the rest of her schedule back in Boston.

And submit her resignation.

It was a huge step, but one that was necessary. She wanted to fight for the right to be Joey's foster mother with the hope of adopting him. She couldn't do that from a thousand miles away.

It wasn't until almost four o'clock in the afternoon that Joey's discharge from Children's Memorial was finalized. Krista had arrived once Ms. Douglas approved the Monroes as Joey's temporary foster family. And shortly after that, Aaron strode in.

"What can I do to help?" he asked.

"I purchased a child safety seat, but it's still in the box," Krista said. "If you could unpack it and get it set up in the back seat of my SUV, I'd appreciate it."

"Of course. Where is your car?" Aaron held out his hand for the keys.

"I'll reimburse you for the child safety seat," Maggie said, after Aaron had left to do Krista's bidding.

Krista shook her head. "Not necessary. We'll need it eventually anyway."

"What do you mean?" Maggie didn't follow.

"I'm pregnant," Krista confided. "But it's early, so we're not going to announce to the rest of the family yet."

"Congratulations." Maggie braced herself for the twinge of envy, but it didn't come. "Does Adam know?"

"Yes, he was there this morning as I took the test," Krista said with a smile. "And I think he told Aaron too." She wrinkled her nose. "I guess our plan to keep the news a secret isn't working out too well."

"You make the announcement when you're ready," Maggie said. "Having been through many miscarriages, it's probably better to wait."

"Oh, I'm sorry. I didn't realize." Krista caught Maggie's hand. "That must have been difficult."

"It was, but I've come to accept God's plan for me." She bent to help Joey into the new clothes she'd bought from the gift shop. They were pajamas, but she thought the elastic waistband was the best option considering his incision. "I'm at peace now."

Leaving the hospital with Krista and Joey felt surreal. She glanced at Krista as they hiked toward the employee parking structure. "I should have asked if you're sure about this. And about me staying with you."

Krista waved that off. "We're sure. And I offered, remember? I heard Aaron is bringing dinner tonight too." She hesitated, then asked, "How are you and Aaron doing?"

"He wants to talk later tonight, after Joey falls asleep."

Maggie sighed. "I guess we should have a conversation about how things went wrong. But I don't want him to feel like he owes me something because of Joey."

Krista was quiet for a moment. "Adam and I have only been married for six months, but we've known each other longer than that. One thing I've learned is that the Monroe men tend to hold back their feelings. It often takes them time to verbalize them in a way that makes sense." She shrugged. "I'd say give Aaron a chance. Maybe he's learned from his mistakes."

Maggie nodded. "They're not all his mistakes; I made them too."

"Ah, the hallmark of a true relationship," Krista said in a light tone. "Accepting that it takes two to make things work is more than half the battle."

That was more difficult under the stress of infertility, but Maggie kept that to herself as they reached the parking structure. Aaron backed out of the SUV, a large grin on his features. "It was like putting a complicated jigsaw puzzle together, but I did it!"

"Yeah, I'm pretty sure there were instructions in the box," Krista said. "Thanks, though."

"I'll head out to grab the food and meet you back at your place." Aaron stepped back so that Maggie could get Joey into the safety seat.

"Sounds good." Maggie found herself looking forward to seeing Aaron later. A vastly different feeling than she'd had on Friday at the medical conference when he'd come outside to talk to her. A reunion that seemed like weeks ago rather than days.

Adam and Krista lived in a beautiful home in Brookland, which wasn't that far from where Aaron lived. There were four bedrooms, but one wasn't furnished yet. "This is going to be our nursery," Krista confided. "You can have one guest room, and we'll put Joey in the other."

Joey seemed disappointed there was no television in his room like there was at the hospital, but he was easily distracted by the very large television in the living room. Maggie knew she'd have her work cut out for her, getting Joey outside to play rather than staying inside to watch television.

When Aaron arrived with dinner, they all took their seats at the kitchen table. Maggie propped pillows on a chair situated between her and Aaron.

Adam said grace, and she was surprised at how Aaron bowed his head and joined in. They hadn't prayed before meals when they were together, but she remembered his parents had done that at holiday gatherings.

Believing in God was one thing; practicing your faith on a daily basis was another. A practice they could have done better during their marriage.

Later that night, once she'd gotten Joey to fall asleep in his new room, she joined Aaron, Adam, and Krista in the living room. Aaron jumped to his feet.

"Let's take a walk."

She flushed and nodded as Krista and Adam cuddled close. No doubt they were basking in the news of their pregnancy.

"This is a really nice neighborhood," Maggie said as they strolled down the driveway. "I can see why you and Adam have chosen to live here."

"And it's not that far from our parents," Aaron agreed. Then he caught her hand in his. "I want you to know I plan to resign my position as Chairman of Pediatric Cardiac Surgery."

"What?" She stopped, staring at him in shock. "Why would you do that?"

"Because I want a second chance with you, Maggie." He turned so they were facing each other. "I've been miserable in the two years since we split. Seeing you again has made me realize how much I still love you."

She gaped, unsure what to say. "Aaron, I can't give you a baby."

"I handled it badly when you mentioned your test results, but that was partially because I had already assumed we'd adopt. I shouldn't have been texting about my patients during our conversation, and that's something I promise to work on." His gaze was earnest. "That's why I plan to resign from the chairman position. I don't want that additional responsibility. Not when I need to be there for you and Joey."

"I still love you, too, Aaron," she said, feeling as if the weight of the world had rolled off her shoulders. Why hadn't she realized it before now? "I love you very much. And I should have handled things better back then too. I should have told you how I felt rather than expecting you to read my mind. I told myself you deserved to father the next generation of Monroes. But I realize now that I used that as an excuse to leave."

"Ah, Maggie, we're a pair, aren't we?" He drew her close, and she willingly went into his arms. "We both made mistakes, but I know I need to make some changes in my life. Starting with you, Maggie. I never stopped loving you."

"I never stopped loving you either," she whispered. Then she reached up and pulled his head down so she could kiss him.

The familiar heat and desire flared as if they had never

been apart. Maybe even more so now that they were back where they belonged.

With each other.

After a long kiss, Aaron finally lifted his head. "Do you think God sent Joey to bring us together?"

"Yes." She stared up at him. "I think God knew that we needed Joey as much as he needs us."

"We'll have the family we always wanted." Aaron spoke with confidence. "Because love heals all wounds."

"Yes, it does." She shivered in the chilly autumn air, moving closer to his warmth. "It's always been you, Aaron." She looked up at him. "I've always loved you."

"And you have my heart too," he said. "Always and forever."

She couldn't help but smile. He was right about God bringing them together.

"Maggie, will you marry me again?" he asked. "Not just for Joey, but for us?"

It was a serious question. She pulled out of his arms so she could see his expression more clearly. "I can't lie, Aaron. I'll be devastated if we don't get to have Joey. But I have learned that we are stronger together. And if God has another plan for Joey, then we'll focus on the next child in need. We can do anything as long as we're committed to each other."

"Eloquent, but is that a yes?" he teased.

"Yes." She wrapped her arms around his neck. "That's a resounding yes."

As Aaron kissed her in the moonlight, Maggie knew she was right where she belonged. In Aaron's arms.

And God willing, Joey would be a part of their family too.

Two months later...

"Welcome to your new home, Joey," Aaron said, opening the door to his house. Maggie released the little boy's hand so he could run inside to check the place out.

"Where's my room?" Joey demanded, wearing his new winter coat. Aaron knew Maggie had loved buying new things for the little boy.

"This way." Aaron walked down the hall to one of two bedrooms that had already been decorated with Joey's living there in mind. The bedspread featured his favorite movie, *Cars*, but there were other movie posters on the wall, along with a tall bookcase filled with children's books. Maggie had taken to reading to Joey before bed, and the boy was already learning his letters and numbers.

He was bright and eager to learn. Not that he and Maggie were biased, he thought with a wry smile.

In January, Joey would start a pre-K program when Maggie went back to work part time as an anesthesiologist for Children's Memorial Hospital. Aaron had announced his intention to step down from his chairmanship position, but his chief of staff, Rob Kent, was doing his best to talk him out of it. Dale Fullerton had resigned, and Aaron had decided to wait until they had his replacement on board before making his final decision.

Still, he was trying to do a better job of delegating patient care responsibilities to spend quality time with his family. Never again did he want to take Maggie for granted.

"Wow." Joey's eyes were wide as he surveyed the room. Then the little boy looked up at him. "Am I staying here forever?"

"Yes, Joey." Aaron dropped to one knee beside him. He and Maggie had gotten remarried in his parents' church and had attended foster care classes together. Yesterday, they'd been granted permission to take Joey on as a permanent foster child, with the wheels in motion to formally adopt him. Thankfully, Oliver Chism had signed away his rights, especially after getting arrested a second time for armed robbery. The reason he'd wanted money? To buy drugs. That had been the last straw. The coast was clear for them to move forward with the adoption as Joey didn't have any other family members.

But he didn't want to confuse the little boy with all the legalities of their situation. "You're staying with us forever."

"And you're gonna be my mom and dad?" Joey pressed.

"Yes. But if you would rather call us Maggie and Aaron, that's okay too," Maggie said, crouching on the other side of the little boy. "We don't mind as long as you're happy."

"Okay." Joey didn't elaborate but rushed over to jump on his bed. "How come I don't get a TV in my room?"

"Because you have books," Maggie said, slowly rising to her feet. Aaron stood too. He wrapped his arm around her waist and hugged her close.

"But you said I can still watch Disney, right?" Joey asked, his expression earnest.

"Yes, but not in your room. And only when we say it's okay." Maggie's tone was firm, and Joey seemed to sense there was no point in arguing.

"Oh, that reminds me, there's a new playground outside too. Come on, I'll show you." Aaron led the way back through the open-concept kitchen and living area to the patio door that led outside to the backyard. The chilly November air didn't invite lengthy playtime outside, but the wide grin on Joey's face as he ran toward the new swing set made him glad he'd thought to get the playset installed before the snow fell.

"I love it! Mom and Dad, look at me!" Joey said with glee.

His heart swelled with love for the little boy. Not that raising a four-year-old was always easy. But he was secretly thrilled the little boy had called them Mom and Dad.

"This is our first day together as a family," Maggie whispered as Joey waved at them from the top of the slide. The little boy went down on his bottom, laughed, then went around to do it again. "Thank you for everything, Aaron."

"Thank you for giving me a second chance." He stole a quick kiss, secretly thrilled to have Maggie back where she belonged.

At his side, facing a bright future. Together.

IF YOU'D LIKE to read another exciting book you might want to try my new Oath of Honor series. If you'd like to check out *Steele*, Click Here!

DEAR READER

Thanks so much for reading my Monroe family series. I'm truly blessed to have wonderful readers like you. I hope you enjoyed Aaron and Maggie's story. This was the book I wanted to write years ago, but my publisher didn't like it. I've updated it now for you.

Don't forget, you can purchase eBooks or audiobooks directly from my website will receive a 15% discount by using the code **LauraScott15**.

I adore hearing from my readers! I can be found through my website at https://www.laurascottbooks.com, via Facebook at https://www.facebook.com/LauraScott Books, Instagram at https://www.instagram.com/laurascott books/, and Twitter https://twitter.com/laurascottbooks. Please take a moment to subscribe to my YouTube channel at youtube.com/@LauraScottBooks-wr1xl?sub_confirmation=1. Also take a moment to sign up for my monthly newsletter to learn about my new book releases! All subscribers receive a free novella not available for purchase on any platform.

Until next time,
Laura Scott
PS Keep reading for a sneak peek of Steele!

STEELE

Chapter One

Harper Crane huddled in her winter coat as she hurried along the snowy sidewalk. She absolutely hated parking in downtown Milwaukee, especially in January, but it couldn't be helped. Her role as a legal assistant at Gibson and Roberts Law Offices meant showing up at the high-rise building four days a week. Her boss, Trent Gibson, let her work from home every Friday, unless he had depositions scheduled in one of the conference rooms.

Shivering, she increased her pace. The surface parking lot she used charged ten bucks a day. The structures were more than twice that amount, so she ducked her head against the wind and pushed forward. The office building was only five blocks away.

She was so busy watching her feet to make sure she didn't slip and fall that she didn't pay attention to the vehicle coming up beside her. Even when it idled in the road, she didn't think much about it. When the back passenger door opened and a man emerged, her instincts finally kicked in.

Danger!

A hard hand grabbed her arm. No! She tried to tug out of his grip, her stupid office flats slipping on the icy pavement.

She opened her mouth to scream, but he ruthlessly clamped his other hand over her mouth and began dragging her toward the car.

The silent scream lodged in her throat as she struggled against his grip. This couldn't be happening. She couldn't allow him to get her into the car!

"Police! Get your hands where I can see them!"

The shout came from her left. The assailant instantly let her go, shoving her backward, then diving into the back seat of the car. The driver hit the gas and careened away from the curb, tires squealing and horns blaring as he rounded the corner and disappeared. A cop chased after the vehicle, but then stopped and turned to jog back toward her.

Harper landed hard on her backside, her arms instinctively curling around her pregnant belly. She couldn't breathe, couldn't do anything but stare up in horror as the uniformed police officers rushed to her side.

"Ms. Crane? Are you okay?" The fact that the dark-haired cop knew her name wasn't reassuring. She stared up into his blue eyes, trying to comprehend what had transpired.

"We need to get her up," the other officer said.

"Okay, easy now." The cop with dark hair and blue eyes slid his arm behind her shoulders. With the help of both men, she managed to get back on her feet. Her body was sore, especially her tailbone, but she relaxed when she felt her baby moving. Should she go to the hospital to be checked out? She wasn't sure that was necessary but didn't want to take any chances with her baby's life.

"Can you tell us what happened?" Her gaze landed on the dark-haired cop's name tag. His last name was Delaney. The other officer's name tag read Greer.

"I—have no idea." She pushed the words through her tight throat. "Out of nowhere, this guy came out of the car and tried to kidnap me."

The two cops exchanged a glance. Delaney nodded. "Yes, ma'am, we know that much. Did you recognize the man who grabbed you? Did he say anything?"

"Why would I recognize him?" None of this seemed real, although clearly it was. If not for these two men showing up in the nick of time . . . she swallowed hard. "No, he didn't look familiar." She thought back to those tense moments when she'd belatedly realized what the guy's intent was. "He didn't say anything. Just grabbed me, clapped his hand over my mouth, and dragged me toward the car . . ." She broke off, shivering.

"Okay, that's fine. We had to ask." Officer Delaney spoke in a soothing voice. "Brock, did you get his license plate number?"

"Yeah. Sent it to dispatch to issue a BOLO on the vehicle," Officer Greer said.

"We'd like you to come down to the precinct to look at some mug shots." Officer Delaney smiled reassuringly. "I'm sure your boss won't mind. We can call the law office from the squad, explain that you need some time off."

Her boss at the law office? Time off? The hairs on the back of her neck rose in alarm. These cops knew her name. They knew where she worked. They probably knew more about her personal life than her boss did.

Realization sank deep. They hadn't just gotten there so

quickly by chance. She narrowed her gaze at Officer Delaney. "You were following me? Watching me and following me? Why?"

Delaney held her gaze for a long moment. "It's best if you come with us. We can discuss this in more detail at the precinct."

Somehow, she sensed it would be better for them—not her—to go along with the plan. Yet someone had tried to kidnap her. This—she didn't understand any of this. Her shoulders slumped, and she slowly shook her head. "This is about Jake, isn't it?"

"You tell us." Officer Greer arched his brow.

She scowled. She didn't like him. Either of them. They'd been watching her. Waiting for something bad to happen. And it had!

With an abrupt move, she twisted away from Officer Delaney, shouldered her purse strap, and walked away. She wasn't going anywhere with them.

"Ms. Crane," Delaney called her name as he quickly caught up with her. "You can't just pretend this didn't happen. Don't you realize you're in danger?"

"Why?" She spun to face him. He was so close that her belly bumped into him. He hastily stepped back as if burned. "I don't understand. My ex-husband is dead! He can't testify. There's no reason for anyone to come after me. To try to kidnap me!"

"Clearly, someone associated with your ex-husband wants something from you." His placating tone grated on her nerves. "Please, come with us to the precinct. We really need to talk."

Her baby kicked again, and she put a hand to her abdomen beneath her coat to soothe her unborn child. She was just over seven months pregnant. Stress wasn't good for either of them.

"Fine." She turned to face him. "But you better be prepared to share what you know too. I want answers, Officer Delaney, especially if me and my baby are truly in danger."

The cop's gaze dropped momentarily to her abdomen before bouncing back up to meet hers. "I understand."

Did he? She wasn't convinced. Yet she didn't have much of a choice but to go along with them. Not if she wanted to understand exactly what was going on.

She reluctantly allowed Delaney to escort her back to where his partner Greer waited, hoping and praying she wouldn't regret this.

Steele couldn't believe Jacob Feldman's pregnant ex-wife had almost been snatched right under their noses. The near miss would earn them a scowl from their bosses, Lieutenant Joe Kingsley and Captain Rhy Finnegan. Both guys were fair and decent men, but they also held high standards.

He would take full responsibility for the incident. He and Brock had been watching her from a distance. He hadn't anticipated those guys would try to grab her during daylight hours, early in the morning no less.

It was concerning to know Harper was pregnant and in danger. She was right; none of this was her fault.

He was certain the actions of her ex-husband had dragged her into this mess. What Harper didn't know was that Feldman wasn't killed in prison the way she'd been told.

No, the weasel had decided to testify against his coconspirators, so his death had been faked. Easy enough to do after he'd gotten beat up in prison bad enough to require a trip to the hospital. He was currently being held in a safe house down in Chicago. The truth would be revealed when they got closer to trial.

Someone else obviously knew Feldman was still alive. Maybe they'd even decided to abduct Harper as leverage against Feldman hoping to get the guy to change his mind about testifying against the big boss, Tommy Grotto.

Either that or someone believed Harper knew more about Feldman's illegal activities than she'd let on.

Considering the way Harper had filed for divorce exactly twenty-four hours *before* Jacob Feldman was arrested, he felt certain she had discovered key information related to his illegal activities.

A theory that seemed to have been the motive behind the abduction attempt.

Glancing at her in the rearview mirror, Steele took note of the way she stared out the window without saying a word.

"Did you want us to call your boss?" he asked, breaking the silence.

Her jaw tightened, but she shook her head and pulled her phone from her purse. "I'll do it."

He and Brock exchanged a glance as she made the call, explaining to her boss, Attorney Trent Gibson, about how she'd been attacked and was being taken to the police station for questioning.

"I promise I'm fine, and so is the baby," she said. "I don't know how long this will take, though."

Another silence as she listened to whatever her boss was saying.

"Okay, thanks, Trent. I appreciate that. I'll let you know." She lowered the phone, then asked, "Does my boss know about you two following me?"

"No, we've never met him." He held her gaze in the rearview mirror. "We only know that he's your boss."

"Yeah, sure." Her tone indicated she didn't believe him.

Brock shrugged and looked away. Steele could tell that his fellow teammate didn't trust Harper Crane any more than she trusted them.

He pulled into the parking lot of the third district police station, then threw the gearshift into park. He pushed out from behind the wheel, then quickly jumped out to open the back passenger door for Harper, knowing she couldn't get out of the caged area on her own.

"Be careful," he warmed, taking her elbow. "It's slippery."

She gave a curt nod and allowed him to escort her inside. Brock followed behind, covering her back without being asked.

Whoever had tried to grab Harper could easily try again. A fact he wasn't sure she really appreciated.

"This way." He steered her through the maze of cubicles to one of the interview rooms. "Have a seat."

She did, then crossed her arms over her chest. "How long is this going to take?"

He stifled a sigh, dropping into a chair across from her. "Ms. Crane, we need to understand how much you knew about your husband's business dealings."

"Ex-husband." She held his gaze for a long moment, then added, "I didn't know anything. I had no idea he was about to be arrested."

He didn't believe it. "You're saying it was just a coincidence that he was arrested twenty-four hours after you filed for divorce?"

A flicker of uncertainty darkened her green eyes, but then she nodded. "Yes. I—he'd changed. He became withdrawn, terse, angry, and verbally abusive." She dropped her hands to her pregnant belly. "He'd morphed into a completely different person from the man I'd married two years ago."

Steele swallowed a sigh. He'd hoped she'd be more forthcoming after nearly being kidnapped off the street. "Those guys tried to grab you for a reason, Ms. Crane. Have you considered what might have happened if we hadn't been there?"

"Yes." Her voice was a whisper. She closed her eyes for a moment, then lifted her gaze to his. She was stunning with her long blond hair and bright-green eyes. And for a moment, he had to wonder if the abduction was for another, more sinister reason. Sex traffickers didn't normally target pregnant women, but it was possible they hadn't known about her condition. If he hadn't been watching her move around inside her apartment, he might not have noticed either. Her winter coat was big enough to cover her rounded belly.

"I neglected to thank you and Officer Greer for saving me," she said, as if having come to the realization that arguing with them wasn't going to work in her favor. She frowned. "Although I have to admit it's more than a little disconcerting to realize you've been watching me, following my movements."

He wasn't going to apologize for keeping an eye on her. They'd run out of leads and had decided to keep tabs on Feldman's ex-wife. He was secretly glad they had. "You know this attempt to grab you must be related to your ex-husband. We need you to tell us everything you know to find the men responsible." He paused, then added, "Before they try again."

"Again?" She paled. "You think they will?"

"Ma'am, you need to come clean right now." Brock's curt tone betrayed his impatience. "Tell us who grabbed you and why."

"I don't know!" Harper's voice held anguish as she slapped her hands on the metal table. "If I did, I'd tell you! Don't you think I'd do whatever necessary to protect my baby?"

Steele frowned at Brock, silently warning him to back off.

"Yes, I know you would protect your baby in any way possible," he hastened to reassure her. "But, Ms. Crane, we need you to think back. There may be something your husband said that may help us now."

"Ex-husband!" she shouted. Then her face crumpled. "This isn't my fault. I didn't do anything illegal."

"No, you didn't." He reached across the table to take her hand. "I'm sorry you're having to deal with this, but it's going to be difficult to protect you if we don't know who is behind this attempted kidnapping."

She pulled away, swiped at her face, then met his gaze. "I gave the names of my ex-husband's friends to the police when he was arrested. I barely saw Jake for those two weeks before I moved out. I—he caught me leaving with the last box and forced me to sleep with him." Her voice hiccuped, and his heart squeezed at hearing what she'd suffered. "Then he got a call and left the house, saying something about how he'd be there right away. I took it as a sign from God and got out of there as quickly as possible."

"And you don't know who called him? Or what the call was about?" he gently pressed.

"No. I was pretty upset, as you can imagine." She blinked tears from her eyes and swiped at her face again. "I thought the call might be from Starkey. Ellis Starkey is one of his closest friends. But I can't say for sure."

They knew about Ellis Starkey who had seemingly disappeared off the face of the earth, either hiding or dead, and had been hoping for more. "You didn't know about the guns he was buying and selling?"

"No." She held his gaze. "I hate guns, and Jake knew that. He would never have told me he was buying and selling them." She put a hand on her abdomen again. "If I had known, I would have left him much earlier."

She was probably thinking that if she had done that, she wouldn't be pregnant now. He wondered how she felt about that, then decided it was none of his business.

Brock rose to his feet and headed for the door. "I need air," he muttered.

Steele understood his buddy's anger and frustration. They were all running low on sleep since the most recent raid on a warehouse in Ravenswood, one coordinated by the ATF with backup from their tactical team that had ended in a major gunfight where too many of the bad guys had managed to escape. Their teammate Flynn had been nicked by a bullet, but thankfully, they had killed three men. Getting one or two alive would have been better, but that hadn't happened.

The bad news was that Ellis Starkey and Tommy Grotto, along with a third guy by the name of Waylon Brooks, were still in the wind.

And those were only the guys they knew about. He and the rest of the tactical team suspected there were others too.

Having illegal guns flooding the streets had led to dozens of shooting incidents, with more on the horizon. As if being a member of the tactical team wasn't dangerous enough. They were being called on to participate in more takedowns and tactical situations than ever before.

"Ms. Crane," he began.

"Please call me Harper," she interrupted. "Ma'am makes me feel old. And I'm not accustomed to people calling me by my maiden name." She shook her head. "I was such a fool. I thought Jake was perfect for me, that we'd be married for decades the way my parents were. But I couldn't have been more wrong."

"I'm sorry, Harper." Using her given name made it difficult to remain professional. "But keep in mind Jake created an illusion. You couldn't have known the truth he kept hidden for so long."

"I won't make that mistake again," she murmured. Then sighed. "I wish there was more I could tell you. Truly. But I swear I don't know anything."

He believed her, yet that meant there was likely only one reason they'd attempted to kidnap her. And that was to force Jake into not testifying. Someone within the Grotto organization must realize he wasn't dead.

He had to keep that thought to himself, though, as he wasn't cleared to share any details of their investigation with her.

"Okay, there's one last thing we need from you." He rose to his feet. "I'm going to gather several mug shots for you to look at. I need you to tell me if any of the men look familiar."

"I can do that." She hesitated, then said, "Thank you, Officer Delany. I appreciate your kindness."

"You may as well call me Steele," he said, turning toward the door. "I'll be back in a few minutes."

As he stepped outside the interview room, he found Joe Kingsley and Brock Greer standing there.

"You sure she's not hiding anything?" Joe asked.

He could tell Brock had given Joe an earful. "Anything is possible, but I find it difficult to believe she'd hold back from us knowing her baby is at risk. She doesn't have any love for her ex-husband either."

Joe nodded thoughtfully. "Yeah, I heard enough to agree with you. Brock, as you know, still has his doubts. Pull together those mug shots and see if she can identify anyone."

"Sure thing." He knew Brock had trust issues from recent events in his personal life, so Steele let it go. For his part, he couldn't help but feel bad about her situation. Maybe because he was still grieving the loss of his girlfriend, Monique.

He found Raelyn putting the mug shots together for him on the computer. It was easier and faster than using paper or lineups.

"I heard the perps got away," she said without looking at him. "I have Gabe Melrose, our tech guy, searching street camera footage for the vehicle."

"Thanks." He appreciated Rae's chipping in to help. Despite being a talented cop, she was always willing to offer her assistance in any way.

Jina, on the other hand, balked at doing what she called scut work. Unless, of course, Joe or Rhy personally assigned tasks to her. He didn't mind working with the handful of female cops on their team, but Jina had a chip on her shoulder the size of Everest.

He grabbed the closest laptop and booted it up. Within

five minutes, Rae had sent him the six-packs she'd put together. He brought each of the three groupings up on the screen, then minimized two of them.

Carrying the laptop to the interview room, he placed it in front of Harper. She looked surprised, then leaned forward with interest to study the first group of six men.

She took her time, studying each face for a long moment before moving on. But at the end, she sat back. "I'm sorry. None of these guys looks familiar."

"That's okay, let's try the next one." He hadn't expected her to identify Tommy Grotto; the guy was a chameleon, blending into his surroundings. He brought up the next group of six faces.

"That's Ellis Starkey." She pointed at the face in the middle of the bottom row. "I didn't realize he'd been arrested."

"He hasn't; we just happened to get a good picture of him." He minimized that screen and brought up the last six pictures.

She studied them, then shook her head again. "Nope. Never saw any of these guys before."

He shouldn't be surprised that she hadn't been able to identify Waylon Brooks. He glanced up at the one-way glass and gave a small shrug.

Disappointed that they hadn't learned much from this interview, he closed the laptop. "Okay, thanks for your help."

"Does this mean I can go back to work?" She looked surprised and a bit apprehensive.

He hesitated. Joe hadn't mentioned getting approval for a safe house for her. "Yes. I'll drive you back to the law office. However, you really shouldn't go anywhere alone." Team members would continue keeping an eye on her, but that wasn't foolproof. If they'd been a few yards farther back, they may not have been able to rescue her in time.

"Okay." She stood and reached for her coat. He found himself holding it for her so she could slip her arms into the sleeves. "Thanks."

"You're welcome." He cleared his throat, reminding himself that she was a victim of a crime, not a potential date. And pregnant to boot. He wasn't interested in going down the relationship path again. He gave himself a mental shake as he opened the door for her, glad to see both Joe and Brock weren't still hanging around.

"This way." He still had the keys to the squad, so he didn't bother to find Brock. It didn't sit well with him to drop Harper off at the law offices, but he escorted her outside anyway.

She didn't say anything until he pulled up to the skyscraper housing the prestigious law offices of Gibson and Roberts. Ironically, their specialty was criminal defense. They made their money defending people like her ex-husband. "Off—er—Steele, will I be safe going home tonight?"

"Do you have friends or family you can stay with?"

"Not really. My parents passed away last year." She grimaced and reached for her door handle. "Never mind. I'm sure I'll be fine."

"Hold on." He slipped out from behind the wheel, raking his gaze over the area as he went around the back to her side. He opened her door for her. "I'll walk you inside."

As she emerged from the squad, the sound of gunfire reverberated around them.

"Get in! Keep your head down!" He shoved her back down inside the squad and used his radio to call for backup. When another bullet shattered the windshield, he hunkered down behind the vehicle, trying to pinpoint the location of the shooter.

The answer to her question was a big fat no. Harper Crane was far from safe. And he still wasn't sure why she'd been targeted.